P9-CQJ-311

PRIVATEER'S APPRENTICE

PRIVATEER'S APPRENTICE

SUSAN VERRICO

PEACHTREE
ATLANTA

Ω

Published by
PEACHTREE PUBLISHERS
1700 Chattahoochee Avenue
Atlanta, Georgia 30318-2112
www.peachtree-online.com

Text © 2012 by Susan Verrico

All rights reserved. No part of this publication may be reproduced, stored in a retrieval system, or transmitted in any form or by any means—electronic, mechanical, photocopy, recording, or any other—except for brief quotations in printed reviews, without the prior permission of the publisher.

Book design by Maureen Withee
Composition by Melanie McMahon Ives

Printed in June 2012 in Melrose Park, Illinois, by Lake Book Manufacturing in the United States of America

10 9 8 7 6 5 4 3 2 1
First Edition

Library of Congress Cataloging-in-Publication Data

Verrico, Susan.
  Privateer's apprentice / written by Susan Verrico.
    p. cm.
  Summary: From Charles Towne, Carolina Territory, in 1712, thirteen-year-old Jameson Cooper, orphaned and indigent, is abducted by privateers working for Queen Anne but proves himself worthy to be called a royal sailor through his writing and drawing skills, as well as his hard work and courage.
  ISBN 978-1-56145-633-8/1-56145-633-0
  [1. Adventure and adventurers—Fiction. 2. Seafaring life—Fiction. 3. Privateering—Fiction. 4. Orphans—Fiction. 5. Charleston (S.C.)—History—Colonial period, ca. 1600-1775—Fiction. 6. United States—History—Queen Anne's War, 1702-1713—Fiction.] I. Title.
  PZ7.V6114Pri 2012
  [Fic]--dc23
                            2011020976

For Jerry, Gerard, and Keith
With all my love
—S. V.

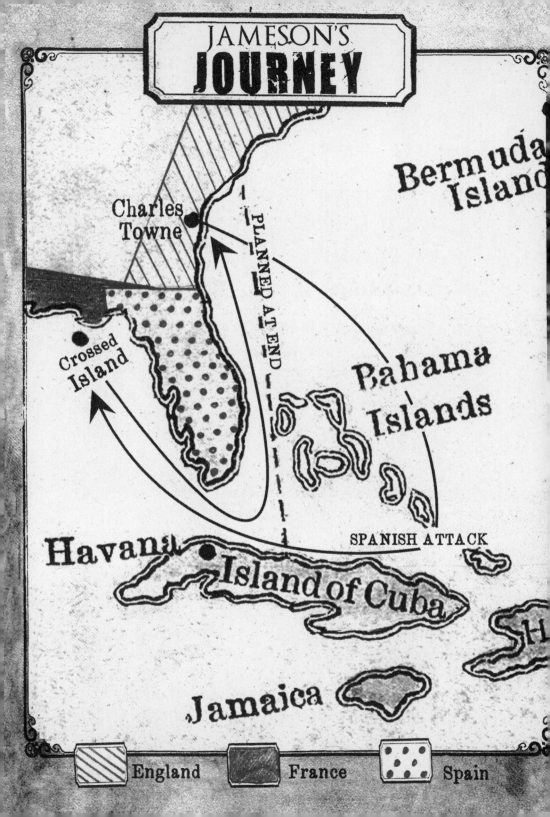

PROLOGUE

The Night before Auction
The year of our Lord 1713
Charles Towne Gaol, Carolina Territory

I, Jameson Martin Cooper, make note of these recent events in memory of my father, a recorder of words and deeds. On the eve of his passing, when his hands had ceased to write, he beckoned me closer. "A foolish man," he whispered, "casts his memories to the wind. A wise man puts them to paper."

I shall heed my father's advice, for memories are all that are left me. Though it pains me to remember, I must start at the beginning, when on a day last spring, my life turned for the worse.

In January, word traveled to us that the citizens of Jamestown were under attack—not by the Indians who normally plagued them, but by an outbreak of fiery, pus-filled sores that brought fever and chills and left its victims dead within the week. Trade was halted and ships bound from Jamestown turned back, but the disease came to us on the wind and in the streams and by the middle of February, fifteen of our neighbors lay dead.

My mother strangled on the boils in March. They filled her throat, stealing her breath and wrapping around her words until she could do naught but moan. When they erupted she spat forth the pus and blood, gagging and clawing at her throat. I stayed by my father's side and helped him tend to her, mopping my mother's face and cleaning away the mess that spewed from her until the afternoon she grew still. Twenty days later, I did the same for my father.

Someday, when my hair is the color of chalk and my back is stooped and crooked with age, I will unroll this parchment and remember the days following my parents' deaths, when I lived on the streets like a beggar. In my mind's eye, I will travel once more to the dark alley where I slept amongst the rats behind a stack of wooden crates. I will feel the claws of a yellow-striped alley cat rake across my hand and remember our fight over a scrap of fat that had dropped from the meat vendor's cart, for I'd had nothing to eat for three days. And though I would like to forget forever that September morning when I walked past the baker's house, I know that someday long from now, I shall smooth this crumpled page and the scent of the hot jellied bread that lured me inside and to my terrible fate will still linger in the air.

The light from the jailer's lantern casts shadows upon nearby walls, and the jingle of his keys tells me the time for writing has passed for now. I must hide my quill and look toward the future, for it is the eve before auction and my heart bursts with fear. What will become of me?

—JMC

CHAPTER ONE

Strabo hangs his lantern on the peg inside the cell and belches loudly as if to announce his arrival. I smell the stink that floats from him like onions left rotting on a summer field. A hazy light falls upon the prisoners who sleep nearby, snoring beneath whatever rag they have been fortunate enough to claim.

"Wake up, you lazy louts!" Strabo bellows, lashing out with a booted foot. His morning routine is always the same, and so I am prepared for his attack. I roll sideways and manage to avoid most of the blow. Still, his foot grazes my chest, and I feel the metal nib of my quill dig into my rib. Scrambling to my feet, I pray the tiny bottle of ink hidden inside my vest pocket has not suffered a crack.

Strabo moves to the center of the cramped cell and pulls chunks of black bread from a sack tied at his waist. He flings them onto the straw-covered floor as if he is tossing bones to dogs.

"'Tis a light breakfast we serve our guests this morning," he says with a smirk. "Compliments of our mighty Queen Anne."

The old woman called Netty scrambles from beneath her blanket. With bits of straw sticking in her hair, she grabs two large pieces of the bread. Still on her knees, she turns and offers one. "Take it, boy," she urges, her speech marred by a missing front tooth. "'Twill be a long day and no supper, I'm sure."

I shake my head. "No thank you, ma'am," I reply, watching the others devour the meager fare. That they eat with such gusto amazes me. Who can eat on such a day?

Strabo pulls open the jail's thick oak door and makes it stay by wedging a large stone against the wood. Light spills in, sending spiders and roaches scurrying for dark corners. Breathing deeply, he waves his arm, marked with ink on the muscle, toward a pale blue sky. "Such a fine day you've picked to depart my lovely inn," he says.

Having not felt the sun in more than a fortnight, I move closer to the door. I scan the street, at the same time wondering why I bother. I know of no one who might come to my aid. A woman glances at me as she passes and then quickly looks away. My face grows hot when I see the disgust that clouds her eyes. *How ragged I must look*, I think, unable to recall the last time I washed. Had I bathed at all since the burials? I frown, trying to remember, but the memory won't come. My parents' deaths have left my mind clouded and my memory full of hollow spots.

Days spent living in the alley like a stray hound have left me filthy. My shirt, splotched with stains, hangs loose over breeches torn at both knees. I brush away a handful of the straw that a stable boy delivered yesterday and knock off a chunk of cow dung stuck to my leg. Pinching a gorged tick between my fingers, I fling it onto the floor. I rake my fingers through my tangled blond hair, wincing, for I had scratched my head bloody the night before, and afterwards, picked squished fleas from beneath my nails. My father often said that the markings of a true gentleman were found in his penmanship and appearance. He would surely twist in his grave if he saw me now.

Cupping my hands together, I spit into my palms, rub the

saliva over my face, and dry it with a swipe of my sleeve. A prisoner, his red-veined nose heavily pitted from the pox, thrusts his face so close to mine that I can smell the rot from his teeth. "Going to a grand ball, are you?" he sneers. "Making yourself pretty for the ladies?"

I open my mouth to tell him that his breath smells as if he has feasted on skunk cabbage, but I turn away instead. Since my arrest last month, I have learned to bite my tongue. And a hard lesson it was to learn, one that brought several clouts to my head and painful twists to my ears.

"Gather your things and line up!" Strabo yells, kicking the prisoners within his reach. The others scramble for their belongings, slapping and cursing each other for grabbing what isn't theirs to take. I lean against the wall and watch. I have nothing to gather; all that my father had owned—the printing press and boxes of metal type, the peacock quills and silver nibs, and the five crates of ink that had arrived in March from England—was gone, seized by a stranger who claimed them as payment of a debt owed.

After my father's death, I shut myself up inside the print shop, pulling the front curtain so that not even a speck of light could creep inside. The neighbors left me alone, perhaps still fearful that disease clung to me. I paced the rooms day and night, sleeping only after fits of crying that struck me without warning. Eventually, a few customers came knocking, asking for the return of payments given to my father for work he had not completed before death snatched him up. I had discovered a small sack of coins in my father's desk, and so I was able to satisfy their demands.

Then, two weeks after the posting of my father's death notice, a silver-bearded man accompanied by Constable Smyth knocked on the print shop's door. I allowed them to enter, for I thought another customer sought the return of his deposit. Instead, the bearded man claimed that my father had borrowed money from him to fund a recent shipment of supplies. I told the constable I did not believe such a tale—my father had prided himself on avoiding all debts—but as proof the man produced a document bearing the name of my father, Jonathan Cooper. I protested that the signature was nothing like his, for the letters looked as if they had been written by a chicken whose foot had been dipped in ink and not by a printer as highly skilled as my father. I even brought out a bill of sale and showed it to the constable, pointing out the delicate lettering that identified the mark as my father's. But he refused to accept it, saying that I could have easily signed the document myself. The constable declared I must pay what was owed by noon the next day, or the print shop would be seized and awarded to the bearded man as compensation for the debt.

With no way to pay, I rose early the next morning so that I would be gone before the constable returned. I dressed in my best breeches and shirt, pulling my father's printing vest over it so that I might use the inside pockets to carry the few things I would take with me. In one chest pocket I hid what remained of the coins I'd found in my father's desk, and in the other, a single roll of parchment with a tiny bottle of ink and a new quill tucked safely inside. Little remained in the pantry, but I wrapped what I could carry inside a kitchen cloth—a small wheel of cheese, several slices of salted pork that I had fried the night before, a half loaf of bread, and two dried apples. And then I pulled on my boots and set out, glancing back often until the house grew smaller and smaller and finally disappeared from view. I had no place to go, and so I walked the streets that first day. When dusk fell, I found a hiding place in the alley, wedged between the butcher's shop and the baker's house.

Grabbing my arm, Netty draws closer. Her mouth moves furiously as she chews the last bite of her bread. "Stay close to the top of the line, boy," she whispers, wiping drool from her chin, "for those near the end suffer most."

I grip her hand. "How so?"

She picks a flea from her blanket. "They are within swift reach of Strabo's whip."

Strabo's eyes dart over the cell. "Line up, and be quick," he commands.

Clutching her blanket, Netty pushes past me and stretches out her arms. Strabo loops a thick rope around her wrists and yanks hard. I move in behind her, but Strabo shoves me from the line. "Brats in the back!" he snaps.

Netty turns to me. "Keep your steps lively and your head low," she murmurs.

I am the last prisoner to be tethered to the sixteen-foot stretch of hemp. I wince as Strabo gives the rope a hard tug, causing the braided threads to cut into my wrists. He cracks his whip and points it to the open door. The line of prisoners shuffles forward and I turn for a last look, thinking it odd that I should hate to leave such a place. However, for two weeks, upon dawn and dusk, my belly has been filled. And on stormy nights, when rain trickled through the wall cracks, I snuggled deeper into the damp straw, unmindful of the roaches that bedded with me. For more than a fortnight, I'd felt a comfort I hadn't known since before my parents' deaths. Now, as the rope jerks me forward, it occurs to me that I might never know such comfort again.

Outside, I squint into the morning sun, grateful for the sudden warmth that floods my bones. For a moment I feel weak with the joy of breathing air that has not been tainted by the stench of filthy bodies.

"Start the walk!" Strabo yells, pointing his whip toward Charles Towne's harbor, where the auction will take place.

I stumble along behind the others, careful to keep my eyes

upon the ground. The summer rains have left Charles Towne's narrow streets pitted, and every step brings the risk of a twisted ankle. More than that, I fear I might pass someone who will recognize me as the son of Charles Towne's finest printer and see me as I am now, a condemned thief to be sold to the highest bidder. I keep my head down, watching only the feet that go before me. I do not look up again until the air turns moist and I smell the sea. At the sight of the harbor, my heart begins to pound and my stomach quivers. Never had I believed this day would come.

Charles Towne's citizens stride busily around Harbor Square, but they pause to stare as we approach. Several children jumping over strewn pebbles stop and grow quiet. I notice the freckle-faced boy immediately. In the bright sunlight, his hair looks to be on fire. An older girl in a blue plaid dress watches him play. I think it must be the boy's sister for she has the same flame-colored hair. The girl looks nervously at us and draws the basket of eggs she carries close to her chest.

"Look over here!" the freckled boy shouts, waving his arms above his head like a windmill. He seems to be looking right at me.

Thinking he is saying hello, I lift my chin in greeting. The boy grabs an egg from his sister's basket and hurls it so quickly I don't see it coming. It smashes into my nose, spraying globs of yellow yolk and sending blood streaming from my nostrils. For a moment, I am stunned. Then anger sweeps through me and I lunge at the boy. But Strabo's knots hold, and I fall to my knees, my arms stretched out before me. Before I can stand, the line moves forward, and I can only grab hold of the ropes and pull back to keep my arms from being ripped from their sockets. From the corner of my eye, I see the girl with the eggs darting toward me. She grabs my arm and helps me to my feet. Pulling a red cloth from her basket, she wipes the dripping yolk from my cheek and speaks in a low voice.

"I'm Suzanne Le Croix, and I'm terribly sorry for what Robert did. He'll be whipped when Father hears he wasted an egg."

I draw in my breath and glance sharply at the girl. She speaks English, but her name and accent are unmistakably French. Hundreds of Huguenots have fled France and its papist ruler, Louis IX, since the beginning of Queen Anne's War. A few years earlier, King Louis had sent a fleet of ships to capture Charles Towne. The attack had failed, but none of Charles Towne's citizens had forgotten. Those tied to France are still viewed with suspicion. Unwilling to add to my troubles, I remain silent.

"You're bleeding," Suzanne says, dabbing beneath my nose with the cloth.

"It is nothing," I say, glancing toward the top of the line, where Strabo is pacing back and forth, cracking his whip in the air. "Please go," I whisper. "I'll get the lash if he sees you."

Suzanne presses the cloth into my hands. "Take it," she pleads. "I dyed it in Yule berries, to bring good luck." She hesitates, and then adds, "Whatever you have done, I'm sorry for your troubles."

I bite my lip at the kindness in the girl's voice. Since the deaths of my parents, I have heard only harsh words. My eyes fill and I blink quickly to clear them. "I've done nothing wrong," I murmur. "A misunderstanding led me here."

"Then I shall offer double prayers for you," Suzanne says.

Before I can answer, the line moves forward and pulls me along with it. When I look up again, I see the black waters of the Ashley River sloshing against a newly built auction block set into the sand.

CHAPTER TWO

The block is smaller than I had imagined during the nights I lay awake, wondering how it would feel to be sold to the highest bidder as if I were a prized sow or a milking cow. Though I had heard of the auctions, I had never been permitted to go, for my mother disapproved of people profiting from the misfortune of others. My stomach sinks at the sight of so many people; it seems as if the entire town has turned out for the day's festivities. Many of Charles Towne's merchants have closed their shops for the day and display their wares on the beach. The milliner has brought along an assortment of hats, and the candlemaker hawks his fat beeswax candles. Farmers have parked their wagons near the watering troughs set on the edge of the sand; their mules bray loudly in the hot sun and swish their tails at buzzing swarms of green-tailed flies.

I know some of the merchants by name. Closest to the block is Mr. Carver, the tavern owner, who used to visit my father's shop every few months. He would make a grand show of patting my head and offering handfuls of candy, perhaps hoping that my father might charge him less for his newspapers. Now he shifts his eyes from mine and pretends not to know me.

Strabo tucks his whip into his back pocket and begins untying the prisoners. "When your names are called, move quickly to the block," he says. "And don't think of running, for you will pay dearly if you do."

I rub my wrists as the ropes fall away and look around, noticing for the first time the nearly empty harbor. *How odd*, I think. Rarely would a ship's captain fail to dock at Charles Towne with a hold filled with rum from Barbados or stocked to the beams with cones of brown sugar from Jamaica. The townspeople valued such goods and would gladly trade tobacco and freshly cut timber that could be used for barter in other ports. An empty harbor in the middle of summer is indeed strange.

My glance falls upon a brigantine moored near the mouth of the harbor. Above the ship, Queen Anne's blue and red standards snap in the breeze. I eye the ship thoughtfully, wondering who sails beneath the Queen's colors.

I shift my weight from one foot to another. Other prisoners seem not to feel the heat that rises from the sand. Old Netty shuffles over to a large piece of driftwood and sinks down on it. Her chest heaves from the walk to the harbor. She has barely caught her breath when Strabo charges toward her, his whip held high above his head. "Think you're at a tea party, do you?" he asks, bringing the whip down across her arm. "Think you can sit and preen like a grand lady? Get back with the others!"

Crying out, the old woman grabs her bony shoulder. She tries to stand, but Strabo blocks her way and strikes her again. Unable to stop myself, I run toward her. "Leave her be!" I shout, shoving myself between them.

His metal-tipped whip catches me across the back. I gasp as fire spreads between my shoulders. Spinning around, I wrench the whip from Strabo's hand and fling it down into the sand.

The jailer's face turns dark. "You stinking brat," he says, bending down to retrieve the whip. "I'll teach you to cross me." He wipes the whip across his thigh and then draws back his arm. I think of running, but there is nowhere to run except into the sea. I hunch my shoulders and brace myself, but the pain never comes. Instead, a hush falls over the crowd. Strabo turns his attention from me and stares at two men standing on the wharf, silently watching the scene on the beach. The younger man wears the uniform of a captain in the Queen's navy: a blue damask jacket and ivory breeches trimmed in gold cording. His brown hair falls loose beneath a blue three-cornered hat trimmed with a scarlet feather.

Had it not been for his companion, the pair might have gone unnoticed. But the older man is an odd sight. Tall and bony, he wears a royal blue naval coat that has been left open to reveal a brown leather vest. His brown leather breeches have been hacked away, ending unevenly below his knees. Speckled black-and-white cow skins secured with leather ties cover the man's feet and stretch halfway up his legs. The man steps forward, and the magnificent jewels, emeralds, rubies, and aquamarines, decorating the patch over his eye, sparkle in the bright sunlight. Turning to Netty, I whisper, "Who are those men?"

"Devils, they be," she murmurs, still holding her shoulder.

I glance toward the ship moored in the harbor. "But they sail under our Queen's flag. They cannot be French or Spaniards."

"There are more demons on earth than those from France and Spain," the old woman says. She nods toward the pair. "The captain is Sir Jack Edwards, but he's known far and wide as Attack Jack. You'll never find him without his one-eyed mate, Solitaire Peep, for they watch each other's back like vipers watch their nest." She crosses her fingers and places them over her lips, as if afraid that mentioning their names will bring bad luck. "Satans," she whispers, "prowling the water and harbors in the name of Queen Anne."

I am so engrossed in the old woman's words, I don't see Constable Smythe approach the block. He stands in the middle and claps his hands. "Let the auction begin! Oldest prisoner first!"

Strabo grabs Netty by the elbow and drags her over to the block. Jerking her arm away, she climbs the steps alone and stands beside the constable, who shuffles through a stack of papers. Finding the one he needs, he bellows, "Netty Nottingham will labor for two years at our Queen's pleasure for repeated drunkenness on the Sabbath. Who starts the bidding?"

"That old crow will be dead in six months!" a man yells. "Bring on someone worthy of a bid!"

Netty lifts her chin and glares at the man who has insulted her. "Old perhaps, but strong I am, and a good cook to boot!"

"She is indeed a fine cook," the constable agrees, glancing at the papers before him. "Take her home to your missus for ten pounds."

"Five, and not a shilling more," Wilton Carver calls out. "If she can cook, I can put her to good use in my tavern."

The constable nods. "In Her Majesty's name, so be it."

Strabo leads the old woman away. When she passes me she touches my arm. "I thank you, boy, for your protection today. Lord keep you safe."

I nod. "And you, ma'am."

Throughout the afternoon, one prisoner after another is led onto the block. As dusk falls, only two of us are left. The stable master purchases the one-year term of a stocky young man who has been convicted of public swearing and leads him away. Though I remain, the crowd begins to thin. Strabo laughs. "Looks like no one needs a scrawny lad like yourself, for you'll bring them nothing but an extra mouth to feed." Placing his hand on my back, he gives me a hard shove toward the block. "Up you go, brat."

I stumble onto the platform and look out at the faces of the few bidders who remain.

"For stealing a loaf of bread, Jameson Cooper, thirteen years old, is sentenced to labor for seven years at our Queen's pleasure. Who will offer thirty-five pounds for this lad?"

My face flushes at the constable's words. I hadn't stolen anything! Had it not been for the sign posted in the window—Boy Needed for General Help—I would not have gone inside the bakery at all. Once inside, I called out for the baker, but no one answered. When I turned to leave I noticed several fresh baked loaves cooling near the window. The sight of the strawberry jelly glistening atop the bread had set my belly to gurgling. My last shilling had been spent on a bowl of soup three days before, and I had eaten nothing since. Unable to stop myself, I lifted a loaf to smell. A little sniff was all I wanted, nothing more. I held the loaf close to my nostrils, inhaling the scent of sugared berries. At that very moment the baker stormed from the back room. Seeing me with the loaf, he grabbed my arm. "Thief!" he yelled, shaking me like one might shake dust from a rug. The loaf tumbled from my hands onto the floor, splattering jelly upon the planks and splitting down the middle. I tried to explain that I hadn't intended to steal the bread. I even offered to work for a day to earn its worth since it could no longer be sold, but the baker would not listen. He summoned the constable, and I was arrested for stealing.

A shabby-looking farmer steps forward to offer the first bid. "Twenty pounds for the lad's term," he offers.

The constable shakes his head. "Twenty pounds for a seven-

year term? Surely you jest. This boy will make a fine worker."
He looks out over the crowd. "Who offers thirty-five pounds?"

"A hard worker with thieving hands is no bargain," the
farmer argues. "He'll steal me blind."

Unable to remain silent any longer, I shout, "I'm not a
thief! I was only holding the bread!"

"A spirited lad," the constable says, forcing a smile. "Nothing a thick strap can't cure. Do I hear thirty-five pounds?"

"Twenty pounds for the little thief," the farmer says quietly.
"I'll cure him for sure."

A shiver shoots up my spine. I can already feel the sting of
his lash.

"Twenty-five for the boy!" someone yells.

The constable looks around. "Let the bidder show himself."

My eyes widen as my accuser steps into sight. The baker—
the very man who brought the charges against me—wipes his
fingers across his apron and lifts his hand. "Twenty-five
pounds."

The Constable waits as if he is hoping for a higher offer.
When no one speaks, he declares, "In the name of Queen
Anne, so be it!"

I stay on the block, too stunned to move. The other bidders
walk away. After the baker has paid my price, he jerks his
thumb toward the street. "Follow me," he says.

As I follow the baker through the streets of Charles Towne,
I try to sort out what has happened. I find it strange that the
same man who accused me of stealing has stepped forward to
purchase my term.

The baker walks fast, flinging orders over his shoulder.
"You'll light the hearth before dawn and quench it come night.
The floor is to be swept hourly, and you'll swat the flies without being told. If they fall into the flour and I find them, you'll
eat them. Each night, you'll go to the stable and tend my mule.

And when I need errands run, 'tis your legs that will tire, not mine. Understand?"

"Yes sir," I say, double-stepping to keep up.

When we reach the bakery, the baker lights the lanterns in the front room and goes to the hearth. He pulls out a long paddle that looks as if it has been soaked in oil. Grabbing a cloth, he dips the end into a small pot and scoops out a thick, yellow glob. "Goose fat," he explains. "It crisps the crust and keeps the wood from cracking." He rubs the cloth vigorously in circles from one end of the board to the other and along the back and sides. "From now on, you'll fat the board each night."

I look around, wondering where my bed will be. Perhaps near the hearth where the smell of baking bread will lull me to sleep.

The baker snaps his fingers to command my attention. "The hour is late and my Sadie needs tending. She beds in the stable on the outskirts of town. The stable master will point her out. Give her a bucket of oats and brush her down." He frowns, sniffing the air. "Wash yourself in the trough behind the stables before you return. You stink."

Nodding, I turn to leave. On a table near the hearth, four loaves remain unsold. My mouth waters. I feel ashamed to ask, but the rumbling in my stomach urges me on. "It has been a long day," I say hesitantly, "and I've eaten naught."

"Take one," the baker says, "for they will be stale come morning, and I have nothing left in my pot for you. But from now on, you'll sell the day's leavings on the streets each night before you get your dinner." He goes into the back room and returns with a candle. Bending low before the fire, he dips the wick into the flames and holds it there until it catches. "To the stable and back should take you no more than half an hour, with a few minutes added to bathe. If you do not return before this fire dies, I will alert Constable Smythe that you have run."

"I shan't run," I reply quickly.

Turning to face me, he cups his hand around the flame and holds it high so that his face is illuminated by the glow. I stare into eyes that are cold and dark. As if he hasn't heard my pledge, he continues. "Have you ever been lashed, boy? Beat until the blood runs down your back and drips into your shoes?"

Though the fire roars only a few inches away, I shiver. He notices and smiles. "You are wise to be afraid, for if you run from me, I will see you whipped from one end of Main Street to the other. Understand?"

"I give you my word," I whisper.

Satisfied, the baker hands me a loaf of the bread, and I go out the door. The street is deserted. Without the day's light it seems dark and unfamiliar. A half-moon casts shadows across the cobblestones, and I wish I had asked the baker for his candle. In the distance, the town crier rings his bell and calls the hour.

I eat the bread quickly as I walk through Charles Towne, thinking about the day that has just passed. The farmer's angry face lingers in my mind. I feel grateful my fate was not worse. Seven years as a baker's apprentice is not such a terrible thing. If I work hard, perhaps the baker might spare a few shillings that can be saved for the day my term ends. And when that day comes, I will find a way to reclaim my father's business.

Remembering that the stable lies near the wharves, I follow the cobbled streets and make my way toward the harbor. When a horse's neigh breaks the silence, I know I am close. I walk quickly, and soon I can hear the sea sloshing against the pilings. Looking up, I see England's flag beating against the night sky, high above the brigantine still moored in the harbor. I walk farther and soon the red-oak barn lies before me. The stable master's house sits just beyond it. I head in that direction, and that's when I see him—a lone man crouching behind a stack of barrels near the barn's doors.

The man rises from his haunches and limps toward me. A smile tugs at his mouth. "Lost, are you, lad?" he asks softly.

I hesitate. The man's eyes make me uneasy. They go in opposite directions, as if they battle over which way to look.

"I m-m-must hurry, sir," I stammer. "My master's mule needs tending."

"Come closer, laddie," the man urges. "I cain't see you in the darkness."

He reaches toward me and silver flashes in the moonlight. I brace for the sharp pain of a dagger's blade, but then I see that the man wears leather glove on his right hand with small nails protruding from it. I back away. "I mean you no harm, sir," I say.

The man grins and cocks his head. "Ain't it a pity I cain't say the same?"

The words hang between us for only a second before I turn to flee. The man is quicker, though. Lurching forward, he grabs me by the back of my collar. The studs on the glove's palm scrape my neck as the man pulls me toward him.

"Let me go!" I shout. I thrash from side to side as if I'm on fire, but I can't loosen the hairy arm wrapped tightly around my neck.

The man's breath blows hot against my cheek. "Stop your twisting!" he hisses. "Your head'll feed the fish tonight if you fight me!"

Lowering my chin, I sink my teeth into the man's arm, bearing down until I hit bone and taste blood. Screaming, the man wrenches his arm away, and I am suddenly free and running into the night, back toward the cobbled streets. The torches in the street have been extinguished, but I need no light to show me the way; I care only that I run far from the metal-gloved man. Up ahead, a candle flickers in a window. My heart quickens at the sight. If I make it to the house, surely those inside will aid me!

Suddenly a searing pain slices into the back of my head, a pain so sharp it dulls my thoughts and sends me to my knees. Gasping for air, I struggle to stand, but my feet can find no ground. The man grunts as he grabs my hair and yanks me up. I stare into the night sky and see that the moon has turned upside down and stars are falling from the sky like drops of silver rain. The last thing I hear before the darkness overcomes me is the man's laughter as he hefts me over his shoulder and turns back toward the wharves.

CHAPTER THREE

The distant bleating of a goat wakes me from a fitful sleep. I sit up slowly, unsure of where I am or how I came to be there. My eyes feel heavy, as if someone has placed a blanket over them. I squint into the thick darkness. Unable to see anything, I listen for a clue that will tell me where I have been taken, but only the goat's mournful bleating cuts through the blackness.

I close my eyes again to steady myself against a sudden wave of dizziness, as if someone is yanking me back and forth. My memory is like a seashell that has been stepped upon; the pieces are there, but they no longer fit together. Some things I recall clearly, like standing upon the auction block. I remember the baker's words as we walked through town, and I see him handing me the leftover bread that I ate on my walk to the stable. Then my mind fogs, leaving me with jumbled visions of a gap-toothed old woman and a man crouching behind a barrel. Could all that came after have been a dream?

The back of my head throbs, and I reach for the place where it hurts most. Would a nightmare cause such pain? My fingers find a deep gash, and I trace it to just below my ear. The sticky wetness of the wound tells me that the man hiding behind the barrel had indeed been real, for dreams bring no blood.

I know I have been taken by force, but I cannot fathom the value of someone such as myself. Had the gloved man mistaken me for a nobleman's son who might fetch a ransom? Perhaps the man's eyes were clogged with mucus and he had not noticed my tangled hair and ragged clothing.

I fumble with the ropes knotted around my ankles. My captor has tied me poorly, and the ropes fall away with only a tug. Kicking them off, I stand quickly and smack my throbbing head against a beam. Crying out, I sink back down.

When the pain eases a bit, I begin to move about in the darkness, feeling for mounds of dirt and the thick roots of Carolina oaks that can split a cellar's floor. Perhaps I am on a farm somewhere, for hadn't I heard a goat's cry? But I feel neither dirt nor roots beneath my palm, only the coolness of smoothly polished wood. The floor seems to tilt as I crawl about, as if someone is rocking it back and forth.

I freeze at the sound of footsteps above my head. Light spills over me as a door creaks open. I grab the ropes I had kicked aside. Lacing them around my ankles, I lie back and pretend to sleep.

From beneath my eyelashes, I watch two men stomp down the narrow staircase across from where I lie. A short, bald man carries a lantern that casts a wide yellow slash across the wall. The man swings the lantern sideways until the light falls upon my face.

"By God, Ferdie, 'tis only a lad!" the man whispers.

When Ferdie steps into the light and raises his hand, it is all I can do to remain still. A thick bandage is wrapped around his wrist. "Nasty brat almost bit me bone in half," he says. "His teeth still mark me this morning!"

"The Captain will split your hide when he sees what you've brought," the bald man says. "Hates children, he does."

"Might be the lad's older than he looks," Ferdie says. He

kicks me hard in the side. "Rise up!"

I don't move. The bald man sucks in his breath. "Methinks you've killed him, Ferdie. There's blood all over his shirt!"

"Ain't dead," Ferdie answers. "Only gave him a rap on the noggin. Might be he needs another." He grabs my collar and yanks me to my feet.

"Take your hands off me!" I yell, struggling to pull away.

Ferdie laughs. "I told you, Jabbart. Faking, he was."

"Best bring him up quick," Jabbart says, turning to go back up the steps. "The sun will appear soon."

When the bald man disappears through the door, Ferdie pulls me close. "You're sixteen years old, boy, and not a day younger. Say else, and when I get you alone, I'll lop off your nose and use it for bait." He pushes me toward the steps. "Get going!"

I climb the stairs slowly and try to sort out what has happened, but my mind is clouded with pain. From what the man called Jabbart said, a mistake of some sort has been made. I push open the narrow door at the top of the stairs, and a blast of wet, salty wind blows over me. As I stare at the sea, my knees buckle and I grab hold of the door for support. Never had it occurred to me that I'd been taken to sea, but the surrounding water and the ship's crew staring back at me tells me it is so.

"Go on!" Ferdie commands, shoving me with such force that I fall facedown onto the ship's deck.

I look up. Though it's still not yet light, I see a face that is strangely familiar. The man is wearing a blue hat with a scarlet feather. I rub my forehead slowly, trying to clear away the pain so that I might think. Suddenly the old woman's face flashes before me, and then I recall two figures standing on the wharf that overlooks the beach. One of the men wears a patch, and the other, the younger one... I gasp as the man's name comes to mind. Our eyes meet, and the fury in the man's eyes brings the stale bread I'd eaten the night before back up into my throat; it spews out onto his polished black boots. Cursing loudly, he orders me to stand, but my head throbs and I can only press my face against the smooth planking and listen to the voices that float around me.

I hear someone say that I appear to be dead. Another man remarks on the blood staining my shirt. Someone yells that it looks to be French blood, and the murmurings grow loud. I lift my head to say that a mistake has been made, that I have been taken against my will. There is more shouting that I am a Frenchman, and rough hands grab my arms and my legs. I feel myself being lifted.

The crew forms a circle around me, shouting above one another in their frenzy.

"Throw him over the sides!"

"Let the sea carry him back to France!"

"The sharks will feast on a Frenchman tonight!"

The men carry me over to the railing. They hoist me to a position above their heads, but before they can fling me into the sea, another voice rings out. "Release him!"

There is a momentary pause before I am lowered to the deck. The man steps forward and lifts my chin for a better look. "As I thought," he says with a frown. "It is the bread thief from the beach."

I struggle to breathe as my memory floods back, and Netty's words echo in my head. When the one-eyed man with the jeweled patch steps into view, I know immediately who has taken me.

Attack Jack can barely control his rage. "A thief!" he bellows. "You've brought me a thieving boy who shakes and cowers before me like a sick mongrel!" He looks at Ferdie in disbelief. "You would have me believe this...this..."

"Petticoat clinger?" Solitaire Peep suggests, a wry smile upon his face.

Nodding, Attack Jack continues. "A dozen strong men were on that wharf! I saw them with my own eyes, and Ferdie grabs a thieving skirt clinger!"

I brush my arm against my mouth, willing my heart to slow so that I might speak without my voice cracking.

Ferdie shifts nervously. "Aye, there was strong men on the wharf, but they scurried like rats when they glimpsed you and Peep. Didn't you notice how quickly the other ships pulled anchor when we sailed into port?"

"Your orders were to find a seaman who could do a man's work! You've done nothing but bring me another mouth to feed."

"I sent Ferdie to the stables to take the strong one who was sold before the thief," Solitaire Peep says. "Perhaps his worthless ears should be scalded clean."

"Aye, but 'twas dark and hardly a moon!" Ferdie says slowly, stroking his nose. "Could be this mate's a tad slow on the grow. Could be he's older than he looks."

My throat feels as if it is on fire, but I force out the words. "I'm sixteen, Attack Jack, sir."

My words hang in the air. No one moves. The Captain's eyes narrow. He bends down until his face almost touches mine. "What did you say?" he whispers.

I step backward. "I-I-I'm sixteen," I stammer. "Since the seventh of April."

"No, what did you *call* me?"

I hesitate, confused. I had simply called him by name—the name the old woman had used.

Solitaire Peep scowls. He taps his cutlass. "Methinks he called you Attack Jack."

A fellow with brown speckles all over his face pulls a wad

of chewing tobacco from his mouth and holds it while he speaks. "I heard him say it with me own ears, and two good ones I have!"

Ferdie raises his hand. "Go easy. What other name would the mate have heard in port? 'Tis a mistake, that's all."

Solitaire Peep yanks up his jeweled eye patch and studies me, as if trying to decide if an insult had been intended. I force myself to stare back at the gaping black hole.

"Methinks he didn't know better," Solitaire Peep finally says.

The Captain nods slowly. "I'll let it pass this time, but don't ever call me that again," he says. "That is a low-down name given to me by King Louis, and I'll not hear it from the mouth of one of my own men." He spits out the French king's name as if it is poison upon his tongue.

His casual mention of France's ruler makes my head whirl, but I do not miss that he has referred to me as one of "his men." The remark has not escaped Solitaire Peep either. He pulls his eye patch back into place

"So we're to keep him, then?" he asks.

"For now," the Captain says. "Let the lad prove his worth."

A robust man with frizzled gray hair steps forward. Though he wears the uniform of a royal sailor, he appears slovenly. The buttons barely close on his shirt, leaving gaps through which his skin shows. "I'll not sail with children," he says. "They bring bad luck."

"Aye, Gunther, it's said they do," the Captain agrees, scowling. "But the lad claims he's sixteen. We'll see if he can do a man's work."

I take a deep breath as the air returns to my lungs. A few of the men mumble, and I hear the disappointment in their words. I know they had hoped blood would be spilled—my blood.

Ferdie slaps my shoulder. "A fine sailor we'll teach you to be," he says, appearing relieved that the matter has been settled.

"The teaching can wait until I've seen the lad below in my cabin," the Captain says. "Tell Cook to bring me a breakfast of bread and ale." He looks at me and shakes his head as if he can't believe such a creature stands on the deck of his ship. "And tell him to bring an extra ration for the lad before a hard gust blows and we lose him."

After the Captain leaves the deck, the men return to their work. I don't move until Solitaire Peep's hand falls upon my shoulder. "First thing you learn is to follow orders. The Captain said he'd see you in his cabin. Get moving!"

CHAPTER FOUR

Light seeps through the planks above my head as I follow Solitaire Peep to the last room at the end of the passageway. The Captain is sitting in front of a small desk cleaning his boots. He finishes his task in silence, and then he gives them each a final swipe and tosses the soiled rag into a nearby bucket.

The door creaks open behind me and I turn around. In walks the shortest man I have ever seen, holding a tray that contains a wheel of cheese, a half-dozen biscuits, a pitcher of ale, and three pewter tankards. Though I have not eaten since the day before, I eye not the cheese, but the hump rising from the man's back, a protrusion so large it bends him double.

"What have you brought us, Cook?" Solitaire Peep asks, raising his patch as if to get a better look at the cheese and biscuits.

"A feast fit for Queen Anne," Cook announces. "Roast duckling with all the trimmings, and champagne from the royal cellar." He passes tankards of ale to the Captain and Solitaire Peep.

I almost drop the tankard offered to me; I cannot pull my eyes away from the man's back.

Without a word, Cook sets down the tray and yanks his

shirt up to his neck. I recoil at the sight of the large mound of pink flesh rising from his back, like a sea monster trapped beneath the skin.

"Aye, get a good gander at it, boy," Cook says matter-of-factly. "I'll not have you gaping at it when me back is turned."

I murmur an apology, but Cook waves me silent. "Me mum, God rest her soul, ate camel eggs whilst carrying me. Me pappy, a sea-fearing man, carried them back from China." He reaches around his back and thumps his hump. "Half camel, I be," he says proudly. He pulls his shirt back over his hump and leaves the cabin without another word.

Solitaire Peep watches him leave, a look of admiration on his face. "When the water on ship goes bad, 'tis only Cook who don't feel the thirst," he remarks.

The Captain picks up a wedge of cheese and offers it to me. I shake my head. The pounding in my temples has caused my appetite to disappear.

"Take it," he says sharply. "When there is food on ship, we eat. When there's nothing, we go hungry."

I take the cheese, along with a small biscuit, and eat as commanded, while the Captain and Solitaire Peep study the paper crossed with lines and thick slashes of brown that is spread upon the desk. When only one biscuit remains on the tray, the Captain reaches into his desk and pulls out a leather-bound book. He dips his quill into a pewter inkwell and turns his attention to me. "State your name, lad, and explain the events that brought you to my ship."

"Jameson Martin Cooper, sir. And I think you know my story," I say, my confidence bolstered by the dull pain in my head and two glasses of ale. "It was your man who clouted me on the head and brought me here." The memory of the attack angers me, and I boldly add, "Maybe *you* can tell me why I'm on your ship."

"Mind your tongue, lad," Solitaire Peep replies sharply, "or you'll find yourself without it! When your captain asks a question, you answer it properly."

"My mate speaks wise words," the Captain says without a smile. "You're right, though. It was my orders, as poorly followed as they were, that brought you here. Still, I'll hear your story."

Drawing a deep breath, I begin recalling the events of the past few months. I tell about my parents' deaths and explain how the silver-bearded man seized all that my father had left me, including the rooms above the shop. I recount the nights spent in the alley and the day I stepped into the bakery seeking work. When I reach the part about picking up the loaf, Solitaire Peep interrupts. "Methinks you're not as stupid as you look," he says, "for only a fool would have left the bakery without the bread. And did you think to check the drawers for gold?"

I start to explain that I hadn't intended to steal the bread, but stop when I see the sparkle of admiration in Solitaire Peep's eye. Instead, I murmur "The baker came into the room; there was no time."

"So you're not above taking what doesn't belong to you?" the Captain asks.

I hesitate, sure that such a question is a test. I choose my words carefully. "Sometimes a man must do things he wouldn't ordinarily do. Sometimes he must do the wrong thing, because it's the right thing at the time." As I speak, the Captain scratches his quill quickly over the pages in his book. I am surprised at the refined penmanship, the letters curling, swooping, and dipping. My father would have said he wrote like a gentleman rather than a seaman.

Pushing back from his desk, the Captain walks over to a tiny porthole and stares out for a long moment. When he turns back to me, his face is clouded. "Indeed there are things that push a man off the path he normally would have taken," he says quietly. "Have you ever sailed before?"

I shake my head. "This is all a mistake, sir. I've never stepped foot on a ship until this day. I'm a printer's son, and for seven years hence, a baker's servant. I would be grateful if you would return me to Charles Towne so I can serve my new master and so that someday I may fight to have my father's belongings returned to me."

"I'm your new master," the Captain says, sitting back down. "And I have no intention of turning back."

My stomach knots. By now, the baker will have alerted the constable, who will have tacked runaway postings along the streets. A bounty will have been placed on my head. I remember the baker's threat. If I am caught, I will be tied behind a cart and whipped. My only chance to escape such a fate is to return and explain what has happened.

I clear my throat. "No disrespect intended, sir," I say, "but you've no right to keep me. Your man took me against my will, and I must ask that you return me to Charles Towne so that I can serve the baker."

The Captain smiles wryly. "No right? Is this baker, your master as you say, more powerful than Her Majesty? Have I been at sea so long I'm unaware that a bread-maker now sits on England's throne instead of Queen Anne?"

"I don't understand," I say, wondering if the man had momentarily lost his mind. Did he really believe a baker ruled England?

"Then I'll help you to understand." The Captain rummages through his desk drawer and brings out a small roll of parchment, tied with a gold ribbon. "This Letter of Marque and Reprisal permits me to command your service. By the order of Queen Anne, I may press any man I deem fit into royal service to help protect the Crown from its enemies. Surely as a printer's son, you've heard about an order such as this?"

"I have," I whisper, my eyes upon the letter.

"Then you see why I'll hear no more nonsense about returning to Charles Towne," the Captain says, putting the roll of parchment back inside the drawer.

I shake my head slowly, my hopes dashed. Even I know that to refuse to serve under a Letter of Marque is an act of treason, for which the penalty is hanging and quartering.

The Captain sighs. "King Louis and King Philip are relentless. Their ships prowl dangerously close to Her Majesty's shores. I was hoping for another stout fighting man for our crew, but you're the one Ferdie has brought us. No matter how you got here, you'll do a man's work, or pay the price." He rubs his chin and studies me carefully. "A printer's son, eh? Can you read and scribe?

"Since I was a babe."

"Sketch straight lines and copy markings exactly as you see them?"

I nod, a burst of pride pushing my head up a little higher. Hadn't my father often boasted that I would make a better recorder than he, that I had the gift of an artist's hand and an eagle's eye for detail? "No doubt I could, sir, for my hand is steady and true to what I see."

"Good," the Captain says, standing up. "If you prove trustworthy, you can be useful to me."

"Begging your pardon?" I ask. "What is it you'll be wanting?"

A guarded look passes between the Captain and Solitaire Peep. The Captain steps from behind his desk. "I'll let you know what I want in good time." He lifts my chin and tilts my head until he can see the gash. "Ferdie almost took your head off," he says. Turning to Solitaire Peep, he says, "Tend his wound before it festers. Then get him cleaned up. He looks like he's already been in battle." With that, he opens the door.

I follow Solitaire Peep into the dark passageway. As we

make our way to the steps, his jeweled eye patch flickers in the light coming from the hatch. "You're a lucky lad," he says. "The last man we took didn't last a day. Tossed overboard, he was."

"For what reason?" I ask, wondering what horrible deed the man had committed.

"Falsehoods," Solitaire Peep replies. "He looked the Captain right in the face and told him a bold-faced lie."

I take a step backward. "What lie is so bad to deserve death?"

"Any lie. 'Tis not its size that matters," Solitaire Peep adds. "A man who cain't be trusted is a danger to us all."

"But what did he lie about?" I press, anxious to measure that Frenchman's deceitfulness against mine.

"The lazy no-good slept through his night shift, and then told the Captain he had been up on deck the whole while. Lucky for us, Gunther saw him sleeping or the Captain would have believed the man's tale. We could have been speared in our sleep by a French or Spanish bayonet. No matter what happens, boy, remember this. Never lie to the Captain."

"Never lie to the Captain," I repeat slowly, as if speaking the words might erase the one I have already told about my age.

"You've been truthful, haven't you?" Solitaire Peep demands.

"Yes sir," I answer quickly, looking away so that he can't see my face. Sixteen I'd said I was, and sixteen I must be. My life depends upon it.

CHAPTER FIVE

As I climb the steps to the deck, the throbbing in my head returns. I pause and lean against the wall. "What's stopping you?" Solitaire Peep snaps. "Get going!"

"My head," I murmur, pushing off from the wall. "It is starting to hurt again." I stumble slowly up the narrow flight. Two steps from the top, my legs fold and I pitch forward. Everything goes black.

When I awake, I am stretched out on the deck. Solitaire Peep is crouched over me. "Stay awake, boy," he commands, poking my cheek with a bony finger. I will my eyes to remain open, but they refuse to obey. From far away, I hear the bleating of a goat and think I am dreaming again.

"Open your lookers," Solitaire Peep says loudly. He pinches my chin hard and slaps at my cheeks until my eyes flutter and the ship's deck slowly comes into focus.

The humped-back cook climbs through the hatch carrying a rag and a small bucket. Kneeling beside my head, he examines the deep gash that runs behind my ear to the base of my neck. "Leave him sleep, Peep. 'Twill go easier." He dips the rag into the bucket. "Twist his head around."

Solitaire Peep grabs my chin and turns it to the side. Cook presses the dripping rag against the gash on my head and wipes at the dried blood. The overpowering odor from the rag fills my nostrils. "Th-that smell!" I stammer, suddenly wide awake. "It's awful!"

"Goat pee," Cook answers proudly. "The best thing for scouring wounds."

Solitaire Peep nods at a goat tied to the deck's railing. "Lucky for you we ain't ate her yet. Cook took her on in Charles Towne for milk."

"Turn him over and hold him still," Cook says. Fishing in his pocket, he pulls out a long silver needle that flashes in the sunlight. Before I realize what is happening, Solitaire Peep's knee is pressed hard against my back so that I can't move. A sweaty hand covers my mouth as the needle pierces my scalp. Streaks of fire shoot through my head, and I struggle against Solitaire Peep's hand, but it's pressed so hard against my mouth that I can I taste the salt from his palm. "Bite me, boy," he says with a grimace as he tries to hold me still, "and I'll yank the teeth from your head when this is done."

Cook works fast, moving the needle in and out until the wound closes. He chews the thread through and carefully knots the two ends. "Only six stitches," he says, patting the wound with the wet rag. "Ferdie captured a man from Port Royal once who needed more stitches than I knew how to count. Never was the same, that one," he says. "Jumped overboard one night and tried to swim to shore."

"Aye," Solitaire Peep says, scowling. "Waste of a strong man."

"You'll be good as new come morning," Cook says. Pressing his palms against the deck, he pushes himself to his feet. He waddles over to the goat. "Come along," he says, untying the rope. "Too much sun'll sour your milk." At the hatch, the animal refuses to go below. She strains against her leash, pawing the deck with her hoofs. Cook gives a hard yank, and the goat reluctantly moves forward, bleating loudly.

I lie on the deck for the rest of the afternoon, drifting in and out of sleep. Late in the afternoon, I wake to find Solitaire Peep staring down at me. "Day's growing old," he says. "Best get washed before the sun's gone." He grabs the back of my shirt and helps me to my feet. "You'll wash in that," he says, pointing to a wooden tub that has been dragged into the center of the deck. "'Tis where we scald the hogs and dry the fish come smoking time, but 'twill do."

I frown. At home I had taken my weekly bath in a large iron tub in the back of the shop, behind a sheet hung for privacy. I glance around. The deck is filled with sailors. A tall man whose long hair is twisted into knots sits nearby, coiling a pile of tangled ropes. A few feet away, Jabbart is scrubbing the deck with buckets of seawater. Above my head, two lookouts cling to the ship's ratlines, scanning the water for other ships. No one, except the oarsmen who occasionally glance my way, pays me any attention. Still, I don't want to bathe in front of them.

"I have nothing clean to put on," I argue. "What use is washing if I must wear dirty clothes?"

"There's a crate of garments below deck that's to be sold in the next port. The Captain told me to give you what you need." He takes a bucket hanging on the side of the ship and threads the handle onto a long wooden pole. Bending low over the ship's railing, he drags the bucket through the water until it is filled and then hoists it onto the deck. "Watch, boy," he says, pouring the water into the tub. "For you'll fill your own tub next month." I lean closer to the railing, watching as he skims the water with the bucket again and again.

When the tub is filled, he turns his attention back to me, glaring when he sees that I am still dressed. "Strip!" he says. "There's work to be done."

The ocean air ruffles my hair, and I shiver as little bumps rise on my arms.

Sighing loudly, I unknot the four thin pieces of leather that close my vest. As I remove the garment, the roll of parchment I'd hidden in the pocket the night before the auction tumbles onto the deck.

"What's this?" Solitaire Peep asks, snatching it up. The bottle of ink and the quill fall at his feet. "What are you up to, lad?" he demands, peering closely at the writing on the paper. He rubs his chin, and then the back of his head, and then his chin again. "Let's see," Solitaire Peep says, his bony finger running across the page. "Says here that you…that you…"

"It says nothing important," I reply. "It's only a note I wrote to myself."

Solitaire Peep snorts. "What stupidness is that?" he asks. His eye narrows as his attention falls onto the corner of the paper where I had sketched Strabo hanging his lantern on the hook. Peep holds the paper aloft and taps it with one finger. "Who is this rascal you've drawn?"

"The jailer," I reply. "No one of importance to you."

"Don't lie to me. 'Twill go bad for you if you weave a tale."

I reach for the parchment. "Something I wrote to help me remember, so that my memories aren't scattered on the wind."

Solitaire Peep scowls and taps his head. "What you cain't store in your noggin ain't worth remembering." He shoves the parchment toward me. "Get in the tub," he commands, heading for the hatch.

I smooth out the parchment carefully. The sight of the printed words makes my breath catch in my throat. My writing is immaculate, almost identical to my father's. How could it not be? Night after night we sat together, my father's hand covering mine. We spent hours practicing each letter, refining every stroke. I copied deeds and letters, drew crests, labored over whatever my father had given me for practice, carefully imitating the graceful way his hand moved across the parchment, so that I could someday help him run his shop.

Pushing away the memory, I place the paper away from the tub where splashes of water might soil it, and pull at the wooden buttons on my breeches until they fall to my ankles. Quickly kicking them aside, I step into the oval tub. The wind blows off the sea, and I shiver as I sink deeper into the cold water. The tub has a strong odor that reminds me of the fish heads left to rot on the banks of the Ashley River. A seagull circles the ship twice, swoops low across the deck, and then flies away, leaving behind two splatters of silver white droppings.

I watch the gull until it becomes a speck and then vanishes, blending into the clouds. I wonder if it is from Charles Towne and is flying back to one of the posts on the wharf, where everything is familiar and safe. Perhaps the gull has a mother or father waiting, someone who will worry if he doesn't return and go looking for him. It pleases me to imagine such things, and I smile slightly, my spirit warmed by the sun.

Solitaire Peep comes up from the hold. He tosses me a sponge and a ball of soap. "This here's the last of the soap until we beach, so use it sparingly. If you didn't smell like a muck pile, you'd do without."

I eye the sponge critically. It is nothing more than a piece of softened coral. The soap has a sharp sour smell, and the color is unusual, yellow with black streaks running throughout.

"Why are you sitting there like a lazy bag of bones?" Peep demands. "If you're waiting for me to scrub your back, 'twill be a long wait," he says. "Get to washing!"

"This tub stinks something awful," I mutter.

"Aye," he replies, "but no worse than you do."

I rub the soap across my skin and it leaves a greasy line. Still, it makes a bit of lather. I hurry to bathe.

Solitaire Peep has left a linen towel, stained yellow with age, beside the tub. When I am finished, I grab it and wrap it around my waist.

"Washed your bum, did you?" Peep inquires, tossing me a shirt and pants. "We don't want the birds trailing us and telling our enemies where we be." He looks up at a flock of gulls, and his taut brown face creases with worry. "They shouldn't be out here," he says. "Mighty far from land, they are."

"Perhaps they have strong wings," I say, drying off.

"Strong wings or no, they're too far out," Solitaire Peep says. "Could be they've found something to land on when they tire."

I look out over the ship's railing. There is nothing except water and sky. If the stray birds have found a resting perch, I cannot see it.

I dress quickly in the new garments. The shirt is fine white linen, nicer than anything I've ever owned. I fasten the buttons, savoring the smoothness of the polished bone against my fingertips. The breeches, gray broadcloth with black silk lining, hang loose around my waist, but a long red sash works well as a belt. The garments are of a quality my father never could have afforded for me. I finger the sleeve. "Such fine clothes," I say.

Solitaire Peep raises his eyebrow. "Aye, they came from a French frigate whose captain thought to blow a hole in the side of the Queen's ship," he says. "We blasted his ship to splinters and then plucked their goods from the water."

"And what of those on board?" I ask, a chill washing over me. "Did you rescue them?"

"What do you think, boy?" the first mate says. "They were French."

I look away. Solitaire Peep is right. The captain and those on board the other ship were French...the enemy of my Queen. But my mind turns back to auction day and the girl with the basket. Suzanne Le Croix is French, yet she offered me kindness on auction day, when others turned away. Rummaging through the pockets of my discarded breeches, I find the red cloth Suzanne gave me and tie it around my neck, remembering her promise that it would bring me good luck. I pray she was right.

Peep picks up my bloodied clothes and flings them over the railing. "Save your boots for when the weather turns cold," he says. "Bare feet work best on deck." He tosses me a stick that has been whittled smooth. Wrapped around the end is a piece of gray leather covered with wiry hairs. "Clean your chompers," he says. "Pig bristles make the best scrubbers."

Beneath the hot sun, my hair dries quickly. I run my fingers through the tangles, wincing when I touch the threads binding my wound.

Cook comes through the hatch carrying a small iron cauldron. He sets it in the middle of the deck, and then rings a small bell attached to the handle to call the crew to dinner. After he ladles out chowder for the others, he hands me a bowlful, along with a hard biscuit. "You'll be sore a day or so, and then good as new," he says.

I clutch the wooden bowl tightly, letting the heat warm my hands. Tiny pools of golden butter swirl atop the creamy white chowder. Chunks of potatoes and carrots bob in the broth, along with thick pieces of fish. Saliva fills my mouth at the sight of the rich stew, and I begin to eat greedily. Using the biscuit, I scoop up the vegetables and shove them into my mouth. When the bread can catch no more, I lick the bowl's rim, unwilling to waste any of the buttery broth. I am so busy eating I don't see the Captain approach. "A hungry belly is a powerful master," he says.

Embarrassed to have been caught gulping my food like a starving street urchin, I don't reply.

"Enjoy the food whilst we have it," the Captain says. He walks over to the ship's railing and looks out over the water. A gull appears and then is gone.

"That bird means trouble," Solitaire Peep says.

"It might have lost its way," the Captain says.

"Put a mark upon my word. We'll have company soon." Peep taps his cutlass. "Mayhap by morning."

"Assign extra men on lookout tonight to be sure," the Captain says, turning to leave. Seeing me, he frowns. He whispers something to Solitaire Peep that I can't hear. Peep points toward the hatch. "Get below, boy. You'll need extra sleep tonight to help heal your wound. Find Cook and tell him I said to make you a pallet in storage. From here on, you'll care for the animals."

"Yes sir," I say, curious as to what the bird's presence means and why Solitaire Peep's mood has darkened. Whatever the reason, I feel grateful to be sent below to rest. I want nothing more than to lie down somewhere and close my eyes. Clutching the empty bowl, I follow orders and go below.

CHAPTER SIX

I have been locked in storage since yesterday when I was ordered below. It is a larger room than the one in which I was first kept. Two portholes, one on each side of the room, shed moonlight upon my bed—nothing more than a burlap sack stuffed with dried corn husks, but warmer than the damp planking.

I slept soundly last night and most of today, waking only when I heard Cook ringing the bell to call the crew to eat. It's as if my body sought to reclaim the hours I lay awake in the alley, unable to sleep for fear that the spiders and rats would feast on me when I closed my eyes.

This morning, Cook left a cloth containing biscuits and cheese inside the door. I did not wake for his morning visit and he did not come again until late today, when the sun began to streak red through the portholes. He brought my supper, a trencher of salted pork with beans and rice and a biscuit to sop the broth. I begged him to leave his candle so that the room would not be so dark, but he ignored my pleas, claiming I would set the ship ablaze. When he left, I heard the rattle of keys and the click of the lock. I think it odd that they confine me when there is nowhere to run except for the sea. I think that in the Captain's eyes I am a thief, one who must be kept under lock and key.

Cook's goat sleeps nearby and good company she is, for her snores dull the silence. A half-barrel holds two rosy piglets that are amusing, but stink fiercely. A tapping of tiny claws along the walls tells me that mice linger near.

I know not where we sail, only that each minute takes me farther from Charles Towne. My heart is heavy over the troubles I've left behind and those that surely lie ahead. Plagued by thoughts of Charles Towne and all that has happened, I close my eyes and drift back to sleep.

At dawn, the hens begin laying. The commotion wakes me, and I sit up and watch, though the sight is not new to me. Cackling loudly, they wiggle down into straw-lined crates and puff their feathers as they drop their eggs. When they have settled, I count two dozen, including a cracked one whose shiny liquid oozes onto the straw.

I stretch and yawn loudly, feeling stiff from tossing about. The ship turned and dipped throughout the night, and several times I rolled off my pallet onto the hard floor. Once I got up to relieve myself, but after stumbling around in the darkness, I discovered Cook had forgotten to leave a bucket. Now, my stomach aches and rumbles.

The goat bleats softly and staggers to her feet. She releases a long yellow stream into the straw. When she finishes, she comes to me and nuzzles at my side. I reach down and scratch her head. "Are you wondering how you came to be here, too?" I ask.

I dress slowly, wondering what the day holds. Remembering what Peep said, I leave my boots where they sit. Having heard the click of a lock the night before, I don't bother to try the door, choosing instead to explore the storage area until someone comes to free me.

Heavy ropes of garlic and onions hang from the rafters, and I push them aside to clear my way. Their juices leach into the air, burning my eyes. Shelves built high along the walls hold wooden crates filled with corn, carrots, and potatoes, though not many, for vegetables spoil quickly; already I can see the potatoes are sprouting eyes. Barrels of small ale are stacked atop one another, and a large cask labeled "rum" sits nearby. Cones of brown sugar wrapped in linen and wheels of cheese dipped in wax have been placed on the highest shelves, beside bricks of salt that have yet to be chipped. Several tea tins hold black leaves whose fragrance mingles faintly with the other odors that fill the room.

I am marveling at the vast amount of food when the storage door opens behind me. My heart skips when I see that it is Ferdie standing in the doorway; his eyes search the room until they settle on me. He shuts the door softly behind him and leans against it. "Up and about, are you, lad?" he asks. "Your noggin fixed, is it?"

I don't answer.

"A fine fighter you are," Ferdie says, waving his bandaged arm. "Got the proof right here." He grins, and I see gums streaked black and teeth specked with brown rot.

He dangles a key on a ring. "Peep sent me to fetch you. You're to hightail it up on deck and start earning your keep." As Ferdie speaks, a piglet oinks softly. He moves away from the door and goes to it. Squatting, he pokes one in the rump, then the other. "'Twill be a fine day when we roast 'em," he says, making loud smacking noises. The piglets stare back at him with wide gray eyes.

Quelling the fear that boils up in my stomach, I walk over to the door. My hand is on the latch when Ferdie seizes my elbow.

"I ain't forgetting our scuffle," Ferdie says. "But, if you mind yourself and keep out of me way, I'm willing to ignore what you did to me."

"You attacked me," I say, sounding braver than I feel, "so I seek no forgiveness from you."

Ferdie smacks me on the ear, sending pain shooting through my stitched-up wound. "Shut your trap and listen up. Peep's going to be hard on you today, learning you this and that."

"What of it?" I say, ignoring the throbbing in my ear. I try to pull open the door, but Ferdie holds it shut.

"So if you caterwaul or do anything that makes the Captain think you ain't full grown and cain't do a man's work, you'll be sorry."

"And you will be, too," I say, "for I will tell him that you forced me to lie, and you will be blamed."

"He won't believe you. He already thinks you're a scoundrel, for he saw you tied like a dog when you were brought to auction."

Before I can reply, there are footsteps outside the door. Ferdie moves back just as it opens.

The Captain seems startled to see Ferdie. "Why aren't you up on deck?" he asks.

"Peep sent me to fetch the lad," Ferdie says, placing his hand upon my shoulder. I jerk away.

The Captain frowns. "I'll stand for no trouble between you," he says. "There will be no fighting on my ship."

"No trouble here," Ferdie says. "Ain't that right, Jamie?"

I flinch. My father was the only one who had ever called me Jamie. Ignoring Ferdie, I say, "Peep wants me up on deck, sir."

"Then go," the Captain says, stepping away from the door. "But remember what I said. You'll work alongside everyone without complaint."

In the passageway, I lean against the wall to gather myself together before going up on deck. Ferdie's voice drifts into the hallway. "He's like a hound sniffing for trouble, the lad is," he says. "I came to bring him up on deck, and he starts a fight."

"Is that so?" the Captain answers. "Perhaps he's having trouble forgiving you the gash on his head."

"He spoke of that," Ferdie says. "He said you'd be sorry you ever took him. Claims he's heading home to Charles Towne the first chance he gets, even if he has to swim."

"Did he now? He should be congratulated for his courage. We are three days sail from shore."

"I reminded him he was in the service of Queen Anne," Ferdie says. "The cocky lad said he served no one."

"He'll serve Queen Anne, or he *will* serve no one," the Captain replies, his voice suddenly cold.

I cannot catch my breath. It is caught in my throat, trapped there by Ferdie's lies. I strain to hear more, but Cook calls the crew to breakfast and the stomping of feet above the rafters drowns out their words.

I am heading for the hatch when a hand grabs my shoulder and jerks me around. The Captain stares down at me. "So you're an eavesdropper as well as a thief," he says.

I lift my chin. "Is it wrong for me to listen when I am being talked about?"

"Did you hear what you were hoping to hear?"

"I heard only lies," I say. "I never said any of what Ferdie claims."

The Captain picks a piece of lint from his blue damask coat. "So says a thief and an eavesdropper."

"So says Jameson Cooper of Charles Towne, who was taken against his will." I swallow hard. Surely I will be tossed to the sharks for answering back, but I will not be lied about and called a thief without answering the charge.

The Captain's eyes meet mine and hold them until I look away.

"Get your breakfast, and then tell Peep to start you on the oars," he says. "We'll see if your back is as strong as your tongue." He pushes past me and disappears down the dark passageway.

I stare after him. The morning's events have brought something to mind that my father once said: a man who permits another to speak falsely about him stamps the words with truth. Ferdie lied about me and the Captain believed him, but I answered them both. To have done less would have shamed my father's memory. Taking a deep breath, I walk toward the stairs.

On deck, Solitaire Peep stands at the tiller. He glances at me as I approach. "'Bout time you woke from your nap," he said.

"The Captain says I'm to eat and then work the oars," I reply, looking around. The deck is crowded; everyone is at work.

"The oars is a good place to start," Solitaire Peep answers, his bony hands gripping the large wooden wheel, "for the wind plays hide-and-seek this morning." His head moves ever so slightly as he gazes upon the black sea. Despite the early sun, I shiver and shift from foot to foot. Peep shoots me a quick look. "You're dancing around like a fool. What ails you?"

"There was no night bucket in storage," I mutter.

Solitaire Peep turns from the tiller. His eye twinkles. "Cook sets the night bucket near the galley," he says. "There's no need for a bucket during the day." He sweeps his arm out toward the water. "Step atop a crate, lad, and do your business over the side of the ship!"

I look around. Which crate would that be? There are dozens of them. Was there one special crate for such business? What if I chose the wrong one?

As if he can read my mind, Peep says, "Stop your lolling; one's as good as any."

I select a crate a few feet away; just after I step down, Cook calls me to eat. The other men have finished their breakfast, and their dirty bowls are scattered around Cook's feet. He dips each in a bucket of sea water, swishes it around, and then places it in the sun to dry. Picking up a bowl that has not yet been washed, he ladles out a portion of hot oats. I stand where I am and eat, bracing myself against the swaying of the ship. The oats are lumpy and have little taste without the brown sugar and warm cream my mother used for flavoring, but they fill my stomach. I swallow my last spoonful and hand the bowl to Cook, just as Peep yells for me to hurry.

He is waiting for me beside an empty rower's bench. There are twelve rowing stations in all, six on each side of the ship, with benches built into the ship's sides. Sweat streams down the rowers' naked backs as they struggle to keep the ship moving through the water. Peep points to an empty bench at the end of one row. "Grab the oar and on the next pull back, join in. Back, forward, side. Do it any other way, and you'll have the ship spinning like a top."

Nodding, I sit and pick up the wooden oar. The polished oak feels smooth against my palm. "Back, forward, side," I whisper, watching the man seated before me. His muscles strain as he pulls back. Clutching my oar, I jerk back as well. When he moves forward, I push forward too. *This isn't so hard*, I think, repeating the steps again. For the first few minutes, I do fine. Then, a heavy gust of wind blows through, and the ship surges forward. My movements suddenly feel awkward. I forget to go to the side and throw my arms forward instead.

Solitaire Peep storms across the deck. "Back, forward, side!" he snaps. "Row faster!"

"It's hard," I complain between heavy breaths. "My arms ache!"

"'Cause you do it wrong!" he hisses, coming up behind me. As the rower in front of me moves back, Peep grabs both my shoulders and yanks me back toward him. Then he pushes me forward, and then to the side. I can feel his nails cutting into my shoulder as he yanks me back and forth. "It's all in the motion, boy," Solitaire Peep says. "Faster!"

"I'm trying!" I snap.

"Then try harder," the Captain says. Startled by his sudden appearance, I jump, releasing the oar. Grabbing it, he shoves it at me. "You're not kneading bread dough. You are rowing for the queen of the greatest country on earth. Act like it!"

He turns to Solitaire Peep. "Keep him at it until he does it properly."

Peep nods. "He'll not move until he has this ship cutting through the water as smoothly as a blade cuts through buttered bread. Row, boy!" he shouts, walking away with the Captain. They look out over the railing and talk in low voices.

I fix my eyes on the other rowers, whispering the directions to myself as I row. But, as hard as I concentrate, I still break my rhythm. My awkward movements cause the other rowers to yell curses at me from over their shoulders. The morning drags on, the sun climbing slowly until it is directly overhead. I row until my arms feel as if they have become disconnected from my shoulders. My hands are on fire. Sweat trickles down my back and soaks through my shirt.

By midafternoon, smoky clouds roll across the sky and the sun disappears. A strong damp wind fills the sails and mists the deck. I welcome the cooling sprays. My back burns through my shirt, and the blisters on my hands have burst, causing the oar to slip in my hand. The pain in my shoulders is almost unbearable. Lightheaded with fatigue, I sway so far to one side that I almost fall off the bench. Just when I'm sure I can take no more, Solitaire Peep hands the tiller off to another mate and crosses the deck.

"You're done here, lad," he says. "The wind blows strong enough now."

Unable to speak, I release the oar. My eyes fill and I blink quickly. Turning my palms upward, I grimace when I see my hands streaked with blood.

"Wash your hands in yonder bucket and tell Cook to give you supper," Peep says gruffly. "When you're finished, come and find me."

Obeying, I dip my sore hands into the bucket of seawater, breathing heavily as the blood from my hands swirls atop the water. My body hurts so much, I barely notice the stinging from the saltwater.

I feel no pride that I rowed almost the whole day with the others, only a dull ache so deep in my chest that it hurts to swallow. I keep my hands in the bucket until my breathing has returned to normal and I have blinked my eyes dry. As the wind billows the sails, the rowers drift away from their benches to seek their supper. After filling their trenchers, they lean against the railing or sit cross-legged on the deck, eating thick strips of salted beef boiled with pepper and spices that float atop the broth, along with the biscuits Cook has prepared. The sun has faded and though the moon has not yet appeared, the day's work appears to be over.

Cook is squatting on the deck, plucking the eyes from a small pile of fish that lie before him. I watch as he flicks one out with the tip of his knife and then pops it into his mouth and quickly swallows it. When he sees me staring, he plucks another and holds it up to me on the tip of his dagger. "Fish eyes help you see beneath the water, lad," he says.

Shaking my head, I back away. "I cannot eat such a thing," I reply.

Sighing, he wipes his hands on his breeches and fills a trencher with salted beef for me. I take the wooden platter and lean against a barrel. I do not attempt to join in the conversation, and though the others cast looks my way, no one speaks to me. I eat silently, staring out across the water and toward the horizon, where beyond lies Charles Towne. When I am finished, I go in search of Solitaire Peep.

I find him under the hull surrounded by a number of clay pots of varying sizes, a length of rope, and a bucket of boiling tar. "Take a seat and watch, lad," Peep says, plunging a wooden paddle into the bucket of pitch and stirring vigorously. Steam from the bubbling tar rises from the bucket. My eyes water, and I cough.

"You'll get used to it soon enough," Solitaire Peep says. "Pitch fumes are a good tonic for the lung mucus." Using a small wooden spoon, he ladles the pitch into a small clay pot. Then he adds bits of broken glass and a handful of bent and rusted nails. He finishes it off with a pinch of gunpowder. Afterwards, he seals the jar with a cork that holds a long wick.

"This," he says, holding up the clay jar, "is a firepot."

"For what?" I ask. I have never seen such a thing.

"For fighting," Solitaire Peep replies. "Raise this up for the enemy to see, and they'll not draw closer without permission."

I frown. "How so? It is only a pot."

"Toss one onto the deck, and the crew will scurry like rats for cover," Peep says.

I pick up a pot and turn it in my hands. "Do you jest? Who would fear a small thing such as this?"

He grabs my hand to silence me. I cry out as his nails slice into my blisters. "If you doubt my word, here be the proof," he says, yanking down the jeweled patch covering his eye. "Take a good look, and don't forget what you see."

I look away from the shriveled black hole where his eye had once been.

"Lost me eye in a battle near St. Augustine," Solitaire Peep says, releasing his grip on my hand. "A firepot smaller than this one smacked the deck where I stood manning the guns. I grabbed it to hurl it back, and the pot exploded in me hand. Took a nail right here," he says, pointing to the black socket. "When they pulled it out, me eye was stuck on the end. 'Twas lucky I lost only the one eye."

My eyes widen at the picture he has drawn in my mind. "What happened to your ship?"

"We plugged the holes the best we could and made quick to shore for repairs."

"In St. Augustine?" I ask, thinking that the ship must have listed badly for the Captain to choose a Spanish port.

"Are you daft? Use your noggin, lad! Had we sailed into St. Augustine flying the Queen's flag, the governor would have finished us off with one shot across the bow."

"Then where?"

"A place what is known only to me and the Captain."

"An island?" I ask.

"Your nose is too long, boy. Pay attention to what I'm teaching you now, and perhaps you'll die an old man with two eyes." He turns back to his pots, talking to himself as he fills each one. He directs me to add handfuls of the nails and glass, yelling when I add too much or too little. By the time the moon appears, we have finished dozens of pots.

Finally, Peep stands and wipes his hands on his breeches. "We've done a good job," he says, looking up at the night sky.

"Perhaps in the morning we'll make a few more just to be sure."

"To be sure of what?" I ask, stifling a yawn.

"To be sure of whatever we need to be sure of," Solitaire Peep says, waving his hands. "Now get below. I'm too tired to teach you anything else this day."

He squats down and begins counting his pots. A frown crosses his face. "Aye," he says. "Methinks a few more will do no harm."

He speaks to himself, for I have already reached the hatch and don't reply.

CHAPTER SEVEN

It is hard to believe more than a month has passed since I was taken from Charles Towne. I have noted each day with a scratch on the corner of parchment that I took from my father's shop. I make the mark and then roll the parchment up quickly. I cannot bring myself to read what I wrote on my last night in jail, for I do not want to remember my fears. The desire to write or sketch strikes me often, for my father's last words are strong in my head, but my body craves sleep more than anything when I return to this room. Someday, perhaps, I shall write of these days, but for now I tuck away each memory.

Morning is the time I like best, when the ship is quiet and no one is shouting my name or ordering me about. I have grown fond of this room, though it is always chilled because it sits so deep in the ocean. The temperature helps to keep the food stored in the crates and in the barrels fresh. The animals and I have become great friends, and sometimes on rainy nights they leave their straw beds and gather near me. I let them stay, for the goat's fur is as warm as any blanket, and the sound of the piglets snoring near my head helps to drown out the rain beating upon the deck.

Today, the bright sunlight shows me how filthy the room has become. Looking around, I flush guiltily. It is my job to clean up after the animals; though I try to keep up, there are many more of them than there are of me. Last night, I stumbled down the stairs exhausted and ignored the stink that greeted me when I entered the room. Too tired to clean, I tossed around some scraps Cook saved from the day's meals and ladled dippers of fresh water from the barrel where it is stored into the single trough the animals share, not bothering to dump out the dirty water. The mess and smells that surround me now make my stomach churn. Scratching a piglet's smooth pink head, I murmur, "Did you come to sleep with me last night because your bed was too soiled?"

Sighing, I toss off the old sail that Cook gave me to use as covering. I grab the metal spade that hangs on the back of the door, quickly scoop up three piles of goat dung, and drop them into the night bucket. A wide yellow puddle has seeped into the cracks between the planking, and I blot the floor dry with a rag that I keep in the corner. I pause when I reach the piglets' barrel and stare with dismay at the matted brown straw. Holding my breath, I dig out the sodden clumps with the spade. When the barrel is empty, I pull handfuls of fresh straw from a bale that sits in the corner and tuck it tightly inside. I resolve to bring down a fresh bucket of salt water later and scrub the floor.

I take my time dressing, my fingers fumbling over the shirt's buttons. Barely have I finished knotting my belt when Cook hobbles in. "Hurry up on deck," he says. "Peep is in a foul mood this day."

"Shall I first gather the eggs?" I ask.

Cook waves me away. "Best that I do it meself from here on. Yesterday, one had the black rot. You must have used both hands to pick them up. Eggs spoil when two hands touch them," he declares. "Boils the yolks in the shell."

I raise an eyebrow. "I often gathered the eggs with my mother. The yolks never boiled in their shells."

"Did you use your right hand and your mum her left?" Cook asks.

"I don't remember." I shrug. "I just gathered them."

"There you go, now," Cook replies. "You must have used different hands or you would've found out about the boiling yolks."

I shake my head and turn away. I don't believe such foolishness, but arguing with Cook is pointless. He is the most superstitious person I've ever met.

Picking up the night bucket, I grab the goat's leash and head for the door. "Get your oats from the pot," Cook says, holding a cracked egg up to the light coming through the porthole.

Solitaire Peep meets me at the hatch. "'Tis time you showed," he says. "A storm blows in from the north. There's work to be done before it hits."

I look up at the blue sky. The clouds are few and white. Surely Solitaire Peep imagines things. I dump the contents of the night bucket over the side of the ship and then tie a rope onto the handle and lower the bucket again, letting it drag through the strong current. When it is sufficiently clean, I set it to dry in the sun. I eat my oats quickly, feeling a tension on deck I don't understand. I am scraping up the last spoonful of my meal when Solitaire Peep pushes a stick toward me with a rag tied to the end.

"Swab off the deck. 'Tis splattered with mud and we cain't be slipping and sliding around like a bunch of fools."

I take the stick, grateful for the simple chore. I have scarcely started mopping when Cook comes up on deck. He is holding a large net with tightly sewn threads. "Leave that for now and help me cast the nets. A school of fish follows us. We will catch our dinner tonight and save what's in the crates."

I take the end of the net that he holds out to me, watching as he ties iron weights to each end. "Lift it high over the railing," he says when he has finished, "then let it drop. The weights will hold it in the water."

We lift the net over the railing and cast it away from the side of the ship. It sits for a minute on the surface and then vanishes beneath the water.

"'Twill take a while, but we'll have a catch come midday."

A spirited wind blows across the deck of the ship and fills the sails. The crew is busy at work. Ratty Tom is on the lines. Jabbart hammers new bottoms on several barrels of flour that have been chewed through by mice. I made the discovery two nights earlier. The mice had stepped in the flour and tracked it over the storage room floor.

I mop around the barrels, dragging the swabbing stick along the bottom of the railing and around the piles of ropes. After several buckets of seawater, the deck glistens. Untying the cloth from the stick, I rinse it in the bucket and place it on the deck to dry. I go to a pile of tangled ropes in the corner and begin unknotting them, stretching them out straight on the deck. I work quickly, pulling and rolling until five neat piles lie before me. Careful not to let them uncoil, I hang them on the pegs that jut from the wall. I am about to ask Jabbart if he needs help mending the barrels when Cook calls to me. He points excitedly at the water. "We have caught us a bounty," he says, leaning over the railing. "We shall feast on fish this night. Help me, lad!"

I grab the net and scrunch it together in my hands, trapping the fish. Together, we haul the net over the side of the ship. When we let it fall, the fish flop around, spraying us with salt water. I feel a twinge of sadness watching them flip up into the air and then come back down onto the hard deck. The poor creatures are looking for water that is not there. They lie in the net, stunned.

"I'll cook some for tonight and salt the rest," he says. "'Tis good we can save the food below, for I counted too many empty barrels in storage last night."

The fish are a curiosity to be sure. Some have long, razor-sharp noses, which seem to please Cook. "Ferdie will make quick use of these snouts," he says. "I heard him complain to the Captain yesterday that he needed more needles to mend his sails."

I frown. "How do you thread a fish snout?"

"First you must poke a hole in the tip," Cook says. "Then you pull the thread through. Fish snouts work good as any needle. You'll see."

Above my head, a large gray and white gull screams loudly. She swoops low and deposits her droppings onto the newly scrubbed deck. I stare at the mess in disgust, and then snatch up the stick just as Solitaire Peep and the Captain come through the hatch. They glance at the gull's droppings and then at me.

"You must learn speed," the Captain says. "It should not take all morning to swab a deck."

"I scrubbed it clean earlier, sir," I reply, not bothering to hide the annoyance in my voice. "And then another gull flew across."

Solitaire Peep peers up at the sky, shielding his eye with a cupped hand. "From what direction did the gull come?" he asks.

I stare up at the empty sky. "I didn't notice until it was upon us."

"Which way did it fly off, then?" Solitaire Peep asks.

I bite my lip, suddenly remembering what Peep had said about a gull signaling that an enemy ship may be nearby. I cross my arms defensively and shrug. "Who knows?" I say.

The Captain's voice is hard. "Answer a question properly when it is put to you, Jameson. Did the gull fly north, south, east, or west?"

"I answered the best I could, sir," I say, flinging the dirty water over the ship's side. "And what does it matter where it came from. It's just a stupid gull!"

"'Tis not the gull who is stupid," Solitaire Peep says. "For he knows which way he flew and you do not."

The Captain glances out over the water. "I must keep reminding myself that you have never sailed before. However, one day I am likely to forget, so you would do well to learn how this ship works and why it is important that you watch for birds and other signs that ships are nearby."

"We are days from land. A bird this far out means we are not alone," Solitaire Peep says. "We cannot see our enemies, but they are near. A gull is proof of that."

"A gull is a bird and nothing more," I say, unable to stop myself from answering back. "Where it flies matters not."

"There you are wrong, boy," Solitaire Peep says. "For a gull that comes upon us suddenly in the middle of this great ocean has found a resting perch nearby."

"Perhaps the gull rested on a log floating in the water," I say.

"Perhaps not," Solitaire Peep snaps. "Perhaps his perch is a galleon carrying gold for King Philip or King Louis. Perhaps he roosts on a ship filled with Frenchmen or Spaniards who would be glad to burn the Queen's property and take you prisoner."

"Am I not a prisoner now?" I demand. "Being a prisoner of Spain or France would be no worse!" The words are out before I can take them back. I brace myself, waiting for the Captain's wrath to fall upon me. But he speaks calmly. There is no need for him to yell, for his words send shivers down my back.

"The captains who sail under Louis and Philip take few prisoners and only the rich ones at that. You, a poor English boy unworthy of ransom, would find yourself bobbing in the water, most likely without your English head."

I swallow hard. "Surely they would understand that I am here against my will and allow me to return to Charles Towne."

The Captain laughs, but there is no joy in the sound. "They would run you through with their polished swords before you could open your mouth. You sail on an English ship and therefore you are the enemy of all others."

I look again at the sky. I know the Captain speaks the truth, for I saw how those in Charles Town treated the Huguenots who had fled France. It mattered not that they disagreed with King Louis; the blood that filled their bodies was French and that could never change.

I strain my eyes across the vast sea. Can it be true that a Spanish or French ship lurks nearby? "Tell me how the gulls carry clues," I say.

The Captain points across the bow. "If the gull flies from the south, our enemy lies ahead. From the north means we are pursued."

"And suppose there are two more gulls, one that flies from the east and the other the west?" I ask.

"Then we are surrounded," the Captain says. "And most likely we will be dead come sunup. So use your head whilst you still have it, and watch for gulls that carry warnings."

"But if they warn us of our enemies, won't they warn our enemies of us?"

The Captain smiles and nods. "That's the smartest thing you've said since you came on board. You're right. The sight of a gull is a message to all that a battle nears."

I look out over the water feeling uneasy. Could an enemy ship lie beyond the horizon? Though Queen Anne's War has waged for almost my entire life, the ocean between the Old World and Charles Towne has always eased my fears.

For the rest of the afternoon I help Cook clean and salt the fish. Cook teaches me how to grasp the needle fish tightly around its belly and then twist the snout from its head with a quick wrench of my wrist; I learn quick enough, but the popping sound when the snout comes off and the spray of blood upon my face makes me sick to my stomach. I work steadily, scraping the innards from each of the fish and then salting the cavity. I place the fish in a small rum barrel that Cook rinsed out, salting each layer as I go along. As I work, my mind travels elsewhere, following the gull across the water to a Spanish or French ship that sails toward us.

When the last layer is salted and the lid nailed down, Cook leaves me to roll the barrel down to the storage room. I turn the barrel on its side awkwardly, wincing as it bangs hard against the deck. I hear snickering and when I look up, I see Ferdie staring at me. His laughter is cut short, though, when another gull appears suddenly from the south. I watch the bird come off the horizon, a small gray dot that takes shape as it grows closer. The gull flies overhead, circles the ship twice, and then flies off without landing. Two more gulls appear from the south. Solitaire Peep sees them and frowns. He spits upon the deck and then wipes his hand across his mouth. Calling for Ferdie to man the tiller, Peep goes below.

Ferdie gives me a great gaping smile that displays all his blackened teeth, and makes a sweeping motion across his neck with one finger. "I'm thinking your head will be the first lost," he says. "For the flaxen color of your hair screams out that you are the Queen's subject."

"And I think I have nothing to fear." I roll the barrel toward the hatch. "Your head is so ugly the enemy will surely die of fright when they look at you."

"You'd best ask Cook if he can find some squid ink to blacken your hair," Ferdie calls after me. "Ain't that right, Gunther?"

Gunther leans against the largest of four cannons that sit on a raised platform near the bow of the ship. His job is to maintain the ship's weapons. Barely a day passes that I do not see him polishing the ship's cannons or laying the muskets out on deck for inspection. He has spent the last two days melting silver blocks and pouring the steaming metal into a mold for making musket balls. Since my first day on board, Gunther has ignored me, other than to order me out of the way. Now, he glares at me and scratches his belly. His white breeches appear too small for his girth; the material strains from waist to ankle. His belt has been replaced with a piece of frayed rope. "Have you brought the devil's luck upon us, brat?" he says. "'Tis a bad sign to have spotted gulls out this far."

"If the devil's luck is upon us, it is no doing of mine."

"'Twould be no one else's," Gunther replies. "Mayhap be best if you left this ship."

"We are weeks from port," I say, "so that is not likely."

Gunther looks at Ferdie, and they both laugh. "Cain't you swim?" Gunther asks.

I lift my chin. Gunther's meaning is clear. "I have no fear of you," I say. "The Captain will see to my safety."

"'Twould be a pity if you have an accident," Gunther says, pressing his lips into a thin smile. "An experienced sailor such as yourself would be a real loss."

My heart pounds. I know if I try to speak, my voice will betray me, and so I let him have the last word. The sound of the hatch banging shut is my only reply.

CHAPTER EIGHT

Though my bones ache from the day's work, I remember my vow to clean the storage room floor. It takes several trips to fill my bucket and I'm grateful that the deck is full and Gunther and Ferdie do not look my way.

When the floor is clean and the animals bedded for the night, I unroll my pallet and pull it near the porthole so that the moon's light is just above my head. I close my eyes and try to sleep, for tomorrow will bring chores from sunup to sundown. Gunther's threats fill my head, and no matter which way I turn, sleep will not come.

My father would tell me to make note of what Gunther and Ferdie said, to pull their words from my thoughts and put them onto parchment; perhaps then I might sleep in peace. But I have no desire to record hateful words from those who would harm me. Instead, I imagine that I am penning a letter to my parents. I raise my hand into the darkness and bend my fingers just so, as if a quill were between them. Then I let my hand swoop above my pallet as I form the words that fill my heart. Closing my eyes, I envision my letters sprinkled amongst the stars, splatters of silver ink against a black sky. I write of my new life aboard this sailing vessel, a two-masted brigantine named *Destiny*, placed under the Captain's command by King William, God rest his soul. In my letter, I share only the good things that have happened since leaving Charles Towne, how I learned to coil ropes, row, and net fish. I tell them about Solitaire Peep's firepots, but I leave out the part about him losing his eye from one, for I don't want them to worry about me. I write about how I take good care of the animals, and how they sometimes curl up near me when I sleep. I imagine the surprise on my mother's face when I explain to her that one can make a sewing needle from the snout of a fish. When my eyes grow heavy, I move my hand into the moonlight, and with perfect penmanship, I sign my name in bold, sweeping letters so that it is splayed across the heavens for them to see. *Jameson Martin Cooper.* I know they will glance at each other and smile when they see I have not forgotten my father's craft. In the darkness, I smile back at them.

❧ ❦

The next morning the goat nuzzles me awake. I open my eyes slowly, startled to see day pouring through the porthole above my head. My morning rituals go quickly, since last night I cleaned the crates and filled the animals' trough with fresh water. Giving the goat's head a quick pat, I pull on my breeches and shirt and hurry into the hall. I notice immediately that the ship is strangely quiet. I don't hear Solitaire Peep shouting out the day's assignments, something he does each morning. I think Peep does it simply to remind those on board that he is next in command behind the Captain.

In the galley, I see no sign of Cook and the firebox is cold and filled with yesterday's ash. As I pass the crew's quarters, *Destiny* lurches suddenly to the side, tossing me hard against the wall. It is then I notice that the ship moves faster than usual. I wonder if a storm draws close. Rubbing my shoulder, I sprint up the steps.

A blast of wet wind hits me as soon as I come through the hatch. The Captain stands at the tiller with Solitaire Peep. His presence on deck so early in the morning surprises me, for he rarely makes an appearance until after the noon meal. The rowers' benches are empty. The sails billow.

When the Captain sees me, he steps down from the tiller and waves his arm toward the hatch. "Come below, Jameson."

"Aye, sir." I wonder if I am in trouble for sleeping past the time when I should have been up and at work. I glance at Solitaire Peep, but there is nothing in his face that indicates what the summons is about.

"Move quickly, boy," Solitaire Peep says through the wind. "The season of storms is upon us. When you're finished below, you can help to furl the sails before we're turned upside down."

I follow the Captain to his cabin at the end of the passageway. A candle burns low on his desk, filling the small room with a hazy light and sour smell. He opens a drawer and brings out a gold box. Lifting the lid, he hands the open box to me. I look down at a set of gold tools. Lined up across a length of red velvet are an ivory quill with a gold nib, a gold ruler, a quadrant and compass, a small bottle of black ink, and a new roll of parchment.

"I'm sure you've seen a sea artist's kit before," the Captain says.

"Only once, sir," I reply. "A nobleman requested my father to order him one from England. It was not as fine as this."

"The one you hold was a gift to me from Queen Anne. She intends that I mark the waters we travel and the shores we find and claim them in her name. England must claim what is rightfully hers."

"And what is rightfully hers?" I ask. My words must have sounded mocking, for the Captain's eyes narrow.

"Whatever Queen Anne decides she wants in the New

World. It is our duty to record where we go and what we see so that she can make that decision."

"And what if King Louis or King Philip have already claimed what we see?" I ask. Almost before I utter the last words, I wish to recall them, for I have no desire to spar with the man who holds my life in his hand.

"What if?" The Captain seems amused at the suggestion. "Of course Philip and Louis have already laid claim. Philip believes that because he holds Havana and La Florida, all in the New World belongs to Spain. And given the chance, Louis would claim the entire world for France."

"Queen Anne would not?"

"Queen Anne claims what God has deemed rightfully hers as the head of the greatest kingdom on God's earth." He waves his hand in the air. "The Spanish and French are simply gnats buzzing here and there. But do not worry; we will soon conquer them once and for all."

"My father thought Queen Anne's war would end quickly," I say. "It has stretched many years."

"Aye, but Philip and Louis are growing weary of fighting. They will soon realize they will never be able to unite their thrones against England."

I carefully lift the gold quill and consider reminding the Captain that the Royal Navy's fifty-day siege of the Castillo de San Marcos at St. Augustine ended in failure. The fort held and the Queen's navy succeeded only in burning the town. When the news reached Charles Towne, many feared that the Spanish would seek revenge. Lookouts were posted at the harbor, but nothing came of it.

The Captain gestures toward a map that hangs beside the porthole. "Can you read a map, lad?" he asks.

"Yes sir. My father copied many such maps for the sea captains who moored in Charles Towne. He trained me to help him. I know the markings as well as I know the letters of the Queen's language."

"Your father did well to teach you his trade. A man desires a son for that reason."

"I would have been the finest recorder and printer Charles Towne ever saw," I say. "After my father, that is." A lump forms in my throat, and I duck my head.

"My first mate tells me that you are quite the artist, that you sketched a picture of your jailer that looks as if it could breathe. If that is true, then perhaps you will become England's finest sea artist," the Captain says. "Perhaps when this war ends, you will be feted at Queen Anne's court and spend your days charming her ladies with your stories of travel upon the seas."

"When this war ends, I shall return to Charles Towne and prove that I'm not a thief," I say. "Afterwards, I shall open a print shop and regain all that my family has lost."

The Captain looks at me. "Perhaps you shall do just that, lad. For I see a fighting spirit within you from time to time. It is a pity you don't show it more often."

"How so?" I ask.

"You do your duties well enough, but there is no spirit in your steps. Too often, your backbone is bent from self-pity. A whole new world awaits you, yet you wish only to gaze back at Charles Towne."

I feel my face growing hot. "What are you saying, sir?"

"I'm saying that you claim to be a man. Sixteen, is it? You must feast your eyes on a man's future. Only children spend time crying over lost toys."

"I have lost more than toys," I say quietly. "I have lost my future."

"Your future is yours to take, Jameson, once you recognize what it is. But enough of that for now." He taps the map. "We are in our enemy's midst. Given heavy winds, we are two days sail from Tortuga."

I draw a sharp breath. Tortuga was held by Spain. "We must turn then, sir. Surely it is a death sentence for us to sail into enemy waters."

"Are you afraid, Jameson?" the Captain asks.

I hesitate. How can I not be afraid? Didn't the Captain himself warn of the dangers of being caught by the enemy? Yet, I do not want to appear a coward. I remain silent.

He presses for an answer. "Be truthful, lad. Are you afraid?"

"Aye," I say softly. "I cannot truthfully say else."

The Captain snatches the map off the wall and quickly rolls it up. "Good!"

"Good?"

"Sailors who know fear fight the hardest. Had you said you were not afraid, I would have thought you a fool—or worse, a liar—and tossed you overboard. There is no shame in feeling fear, Jameson. It is an honest feeling."

"Will we be fighting soon, then?" I ask. My throat suddenly feels dry, and I swallow hard.

"We will likely not advance many more days without encountering a Spanish ship. Havana and the islands surrounding her are well protected." He holds up the golden nib so that the light reflects off it. "With a shortage of crew, I have been unable to find a sea-artist for *Destiny,* and I have neglected my duties to Queen Anne. So, I am turning this kit over to you, Jameson. From here on, you will serve as *Destiny's* sea artist."

"And what shall I draw?" I ask.

"Land," the Captain says. "We must bring Queen Anne maps of all we survey from here to the Carolinas. From these maps, she will select where she wants to establish a hold. We will sail as close to the shore as possible over the next few days. You are to sit on the deck and sketch what you see. Read the compass and record the markings."

"And if I see signs that the Spanish are nearby?" I ask.

The Captain laughs. "You will not have to look hard to see

that. They will see us before we see them. Do not worry, though. They will let us pass." He places the lid back on the box. "I'm entrusting you with this, Jameson. Watch over it well."

My head swirls with questions. I want to ask why we are deliberately sailing into enemy territory. If the Captain knows a Spanish ship lies ahead, why does he not order *Destiny* turned? And why would King Philip's sailors not attack *Destiny*? Frustrated, I sigh. Nothing the Captain has said makes any sense.

I spend the rest of the morning with him as he shows me how to read the compass and how to record what I see. When I make a mistake, he simply shakes his head and tells me to look at the compass again. From time to time he smiles, and I know he is pleased by the way I learn so quickly. Finally, he says, "Go above now and tell Peep that we have spoken and that he will need to assign another to furl the sails; you are to begin your new duties immediately." He turns away, and I realize I have been dismissed.

Up on deck, I find the first mate and tell him what the Captain said. Peep nods. "You'll serve as another lookout, boy. Were the ship full crew, we would have lookouts at every point, but we must make do with what we have. Cook is working with Jabbart and Gunther to prepare the weapons and shot. Ferdie is checking the rigging and sails. The rest of the crew will keep their eyes and ears alert as they perform their jobs. We must be ready!"

"Where shall I sit?" I ask.

Peep looks around. "Start at port," he replies. "When the sun begins to wane, shift to starboard. If you see anything that raises your hair, sound an alarm."

My stomach rumbles loudly. Solitaire Peep lifts an eyebrow. "You've not yet broken your fast?"

I shake my head. "The ash box is cold. I can wait for the noon meal."

"There will be no noon meal," Solitaire Peep says. "With the ship moving so quickly, Cook cannot light a fire and risk sending an ember into the sails. Grab a biscuit and a piece of dried meat. Cold meals will have to do for the next day or so."

As I head below to the galley, the ship's flag snaps loudly in the wind. I look up, squinting against the sun's haze. What I see causes me to gasp. Flying high above the ship is not England's banner, but rather that of Spain.

CHAPTER NINE

I recoil at the sight of the rearing crowned lions on the enemy's flag. Surely the sun has caused my eyes to play tricks on me. But it is no illusion. The image is real.

I can think of no reason for the symbol of the Spanish throne to fly above Queen Anne's ship. Leaning against the railing, I stare hard at the banner, my mind clouded with confusion. Only minutes ago, I heard the Captain proclaim loyalty to Queen Anne, yet he now allows the Spanish flag to fly above her ship. It makes no sense; even worse, it is dangerous. "It is treason," I whisper, shaking my head. I turn on my heels and cross the deck. Solitaire Peep will have the answers I seek.

He looks up from the tiller as I approach. "Why haven't you started your sketching, boy?" he asks. "You're wasting time!"

"I must first ask you something."

"I have no time for learning you today, lad," Solitaire Peep says. "Me eye must be on the waters and the sky. Take your questions elsewhere."

"I bring them to you because you know all that happens on this ship and all that the Captain does." I feel fear rise in me. I had thought my situation could not grow much worse, but surely taking part in a treasonous act is more dangerous than anything I could have imagined.

"'Tis true," Solitaire Peep says. He seems pleased by my flattery. "Ask your questions, then."

"Our Captain professes loyalty to England and our Queen. He commands that I sketch what I see, so Queen Anne can claim what is rightfully hers. I must know why it appears as if he has betrayed her."

"You waste my time spewing nonsense, lad," Solitaire Peep says. His voice is low and sharp. "Our Captain's loyalty runs to the bone and cannot be questioned. Wag your tongue loosely and mayhap you'll find yourself without it."

I persist. "King Philip's flag has been raised and Queen Anne's lowered. The Captain has declared *Destiny* under Spanish rule, and I must know why."

Solitaire Peep sighs heavily. "Your stupidness grows tiresome, boy. You must learn to use your head as a sailor would. We are in Spanish waters. 'Twould be a cry for death to sail through flying the Cross."

My eyes widen as Solitaire Peep's words sink in. A ruse to fool the enemy; I had never considered such a thing. "We pose as Spaniards, then," I say, a smile tugging at my mouth. "A brilliant idea!"

"Aye," Solitaire Peep agrees. "In the Captain's cabin is a chest with flags from every nation. In spring when we sail toward New France, we will hoist King Louis's colors. Does that quell your wondering?"

I nod, embarrassed I hadn't figured it out on my own. Solitaire Peep is right. From here on, I must try to think as a sailor would.

Satisfied with the answers I have been given, I grab some biscuits from the galley and hurry back on deck. I position myself near the bow and place the compass beside me. When the needle grows still, I begin to sketch a series of lines, first up and down, then across, trying to record the ship's position in the way that the Captain taught me.

I look out over the water, unsure of what to draw next. Nothing lies before me except a bright blue sea. Surely the Captain meant for me to draw more than water.

The hours drag. As the sun grows stronger, I struggle to keep my eyes open. It feels if someone has placed a weight around my neck, and I let my head rest against the railing. I'm not sure how long I've slept when I'm awakened by a sound—the cawing of a bird—that causes me to jerk my head upright.

I scan the sky but see nothing. Could I have dreamed the bird's cry? I wait, but the sound doesn't come again. Slowly, though, signs that we are nearing land begin to appear. Leaves and bits of broken limbs and bark float past. I call to Solitaire Peep to point out what I see. "Keep looking, boy," he says. "You will soon see more than that."

Then, just as the sun is starting to sink in the sky, a shore-line appears on the horizon. *Destiny* turns and gains speed, and I realize Solitaire Peep is going to run the ship along the shore. The urge to glimpse land overwhelms me, and I stand for a better look. My hair, bleached white from the sun, blows back from my face and sprays of salt water sting my eyes, but I don't care. For the first time in weeks, land is in sight. Nothing else matters.

Standing on my toes, I lean far over the ship's side, holding tightly to the railing to steady myself. I can see stumps of felled trees and dried seaweed strewn about the beach. The muddy scent of wet earth fills my nostrils, and I breathe in hard and close my eyes. They are still shut when Gunther leaves the cannons and charges across the deck. He grabs me by the shoulder and slings me away from the railing. "Get down, you fool!"

The edge of the rigging platform cuts into my back as I fall against it.

"Have you lost your mind, brat?" Gunther asks, looming

over me. "Your flaxen locks will give us away!" Gunther's hair has come loose from the tails he usually wears, and it blows wildly about his face like swarms of skinny black snakes.

I scramble to my feet, fists raised. "Keep your hands off me!"

Gunther leans in close. "I should kill you now," he taunts. "You'll lead us to death for sure."

"If you kill me, you will hang," I say, not bothering to lower my voice. "On land or ship, murder is a hanging crime."

"'Tis," Gunther says. "But I'll not swing over the likes of you. A ship is a dangerous place." He nods toward the tiller. "Old One-Eye's proof of that."

"The Captain has ordered that I serve as the ship's sea artist," I say. My chest heaves, but my voice sounds strong, and I am glad for that. "What accident will I have? Might I pierce a finger with my quill and bleed to death? Or do you hope the parchment will suddenly rise up like a serpent and strike my nose?" I force a laugh. "Take your threats elsewhere. You cannot harm me."

Gunther grabs my wrist and wrenches it until the quill clatters onto the deck. "Do not mock me, brat," he whispers. "I will pick my teeth with your lanky bones before this voyage is out."

"You have no teeth to pick," I say, lifting my head defiantly.

Gunther's eyes open wide at the insult, and he twists my arm until I gasp in pain. No doubt he would have snapped it in half if Ratty Tom had not cried out suddenly.

"Ship ahead! Ship full ahead!"

The ship turns sharply in the water as the front rowers drop their oars and grab for the muskets and pistols beside their benches. Gunther knocks me aside and runs to the cannons. Someone clangs the ship's bell five times to signal the approach of another ship. The last bell still echoes when the

Captain charges onto the deck. He shouts skyward. "Can you call the flag?"

Ratty Tom raises his eyeglass. "Aye," he says, "she sails for Philip."

"Head for shore, Captain?" Gunther asks.

The Captain shakes his head. "We'll hold steady. When they see we fly their king's colors they will not pursue."

I bend to pick up the quill, my stomach churning. Did the Spanish ship's lookout see me hanging over the sides of the ship? Have I betrayed *Destiny*'s cover? The confidence I had felt earlier disappears Will my head float on the water come next dawn? My eyes strain to see across the water, but I can see nothing. The enemy vessel is still too far away to know if the Captain's ruse has worked.

For the remainder of the evening, the Captain stays on deck, never moving far from Solitaire Peep's side. Few words pass between them and those that do are for their ears only.

When the first stars appear, Cook brings the goat up on deck. She bleats for attention. "Can you milk her, lad?" Cook asks. "Supper's late and the men will start bellowing if their bellies ain't full."

I take the bailing pail from the hook. The goat stands still while I milk, her trust in me sealed by the pieces of rotting vegetables I slip her each morning.

To ease the crew's nerves, the Captain orders a cask of small ale be brought up from the storage room. Cups are passed around, along with cold slabs of biscuit. I pour the goat's milk into an earthen jug, take my portion of food and ale, and go back to my station.

Soon, the Spanish vessel's shadow falls upon the water beneath the full moon. I can't be certain without an eyeglass, but it looks to be a four-masted merchant. Such ships carry large crews and can hold many prisoners. *Destiny* cannot fight off such a ship.

Gunther has not come near me since the cry rang out. He is too busy preparing the weapons. He has gathered a collection of muskets and flintlocks, pikes, daggers, and small bags of grapeshot for the cannons, as well as the firepots Solitaire Peep made. Occasionally, he glances my way, but with the Captain on deck, he keeps silent. When our eyes meet, I see hatred.

At midnight, Jabbart clangs the bell twice to summon a change of watchmen. Solitaire Peep jerks his thumb at me. "Get some sleep, boy," he says. "You'll need it come morning."

I cannot fathom sleeping while an enemy ship lies so near. "I shall stay on deck for a while," I say.

"There is no need for you up here. Get below!" Peep commands.

Gunther has left the cannons to refill his cup with ale. He grins lopsidedly and points up to the man on the riggings. "Let the brat relieve Ratty Tom," he says. "If he ain't tired, let him work."

Solitaire Peep raises an eyebrow. "Methinks not. He can barely climb a ladder without pitching forward."

Gunther slurps loudly from his cup. "Worthless as driftwood," he says.

I lift my chin at Peep's reminder of my first day aboard ship when I fell on the stairs. "My head is healed," I say. "I can climb as good as any man."

"Mayhap some other day when the enemy isn't near," Solitaire Peep says, dismissing me with a wave of his hand. "We have no time to fish you out of the water this night."

"If the lad hangs on like I tell him, he won't fall," Gunther says. "What use is a sailor who cain't climb the ratlines? Every man works onboard *Destiny*. Ain't that right, Captain?" Gunther's voice holds a challenge that is evident to all. Several of the crew stop what they are doing and listen.

The Captain doesn't answer right away. He turns from the railing and gestures to Solitaire Peep. "Let Jameson try the lines," he says. "It is time he learned. He can see as well as any if the ship turns toward us."

Solitaire Peep quickly waves Ratty Tom down. I watch intently as he swings off from the ship's tallest yard and scrambles down the lines, one hand over the other, his feet hooking the rigging. *It doesn't look too hard*, I say to myself, as the man drops with a loud thud onto the deck.

"Think you can do it, lad?" Solitaire Peep asks, handing me the eyeglass.

I nod. I have no choice now.

"Loop a rope around his waist," the Captain says to Gunther. "Keep a tight hold on the end should the lad stumble."

Gunther snorts loudly. "The other mates go it alone."

"I need no rope," I say quickly.

"Do not question me," the Captain says, his voice as cold as the night's wind. "Loop the rope as I say."

"Tie it around him!" Solitaire Peep picks up a rope from the ship's deck and tosses it to Gunther. "You put us at risk with your whining."

I hold my breath and look over Gunther's shoulder as he wraps the thick roping around my waist.

"Keep your eyes skyward," Solitaire Peep says.

The eyeglass in my pocket bumps against my leg as I start up the ropes.

One hand above the other, then the feet, then the hands, I think as I carefully work my way up the rigging. Halfway up, my foot slips and I kick frantically, trying to latch onto the ropes. Forgetting Solitaire Peep's warning, I look down into the rolling black sea. The biscuit I ate earlier surges into my throat. I cling to the lines, unable to go any farther.

"Keep going!" Solitaire Peep yells. "Get on the lines before the other ship is upon us!"

I am frozen, unable to think. Flushes of heat flood my body. My hands grow moist and slide on the rope. I tighten my grip. Swallowing hard, I look up and am dismayed to see that I have made it only halfway up to the yard. I try again to move up, but my hands refuse to let go of the rope.

"The lad's scared," Gunther says, laughing. "Might be he needs me to come up and carry him down like a babe in arms." He shouts to me. "Want me to fetch you down, laddie?"

"Shall I send him up, Jameson?" the Captain yells. "Do you need to be carried down?"

Breathing hard, I shout back, "I have a cramp in my side, that is all!"

Tears sting my eyes. I want to believe they are from the wind. I blink fast and swallow the bile that has filled my mouth. Slowly, I lift my foot from the rope and place it on the one above it. Without thinking of what I am doing, or what lies beneath me, I continue upward. Finally, I reach the top. The yard swings before me, and I grab it and wrap my arms around it. My breath comes in small gasps.

"Can you see the other ship?" the Captain calls.

Holding on tightly with one hand, I carefully pull the eye-glass from my pocket and raise it to my eye. The moon's glow lights the water. My heart beats faster as the Spanish ship looms into view.

"Aye!" I yell. Ashamed at the quake in my voice, I clear my throat and add, "She's a Spanish merchant to be sure. King Philip's flag waves strong."

"Can you count the cannons?" Gunther shouts.

The question is a ridiculous one, for most merchants carry a half-dozen or more. Gunther is asking so that I am forced to hang one-handed from the rigging. Muttering beneath my breath, I begin counting. "Eight, perhaps ten!" I yell down. "She dips in the water and I cannot be sure."

"We must know if she turns," Solitaire Peep says. "Settle in and keep an eye on her. 'Twill be a long night, for sure."

Fear of falling into the churning sea overcomes my need

for sleep. I wrap my arm through the lines attached to the mast and lean against it as I watch through the eyeglass. I gauge the passage of time by the rising moon. From time to time, passing clouds blot out the moonlight, and I am left in darkness. As the night deepens, the wind grows stronger and skims the water. I use my sleeve to wipe the spray from my face and blow hot air from my mouth to warm my hands. The noise on the ship grows dim until only the whistle of the wind blowing between the sails breaks the silence. I know that below me, others watch and listen, for the Captain would never put the safety of his ship into only my hands, but I feel proud that I am *Destiny*'s chief lookout on a night when the enemy is near.

With the eyeglass, I find the hull of the Spanish merchant. In the darkness, I cannot see more than shadows, but I wonder if across the way, a sailor stares back, waiting for *Destiny* to make the first move. Below me, I hear Gunther's voice, and my mind turns back to the moment earlier when I spotted land and ran to the railing. Though I hate to admit that Gunther is right, I had put the ship at risk. When this night is over, I vow to ask Cook if we can try to net a squid. If we do, I'll rub its ink from root to end so my hair won't announce my English blood.

When dawn breaks, the Spanish ship still has not drawn closer. I hear voices below me as the crew wakes. Curiosity draws my eyes downward and I see Gunther yawning and stretching near the cannons. He stumbles to his feet as the Captain comes over to inspect the guns.

"Climb down, lad," Solitaire Peep calls to me. "You've done a good job."

Peep's praise and a night spent hanging on the rigging have boosted my confidence. I place the eyeglass securely in my pocket and start down the roping. My legs feel stiff, and I stop for a minute to let the blood flow back into them. Soon, though, I am moving nimbly along as if I have climbed the lines my entire life. I sense those on deck watching me, and I am glad. Perhaps now they will see I am an able sailor.

The wind is strong, and every now and then I have to stop until it dies down enough for me to go on. When I have made it almost to the bottom, I pause and glance down to gauge the distance from the ropes to the deck. Only a few feet remain from where I need to let go. I envision Ratty Tom's jump, how he had leaned sideways toward the deck as he neared, so that he had a clear landing. I take a deep breath and move my hands to the outside of the ropes so that they don't get tangled when I make the leap. I feel a slight tugging at the ropes at my waist that causes me to look down. Gunther is staring up at me. Our eyes meet, and I see a smile playing on his mouth. "Watch your step, lad!" he yells up to me. "There's sharks at port!"

His words startle me, and I jerk back awkwardly. One foot slips from the roping, throwing me off balance. I kick frantically to find something for my foot to grip, but the wind pushes my body outward like a sheet flapping on a line. I feel the safety tether slipping from my waist, but there is nothing I can do to stop it. Below me, I hear Solitaire Peep shouting, and then I hear the Captain shouting too, but their words are lost on the wind. My arms feel as if they are being pulled from the sockets as the weight of my body pulls me downward. I try to tighten my grip but I can't hold on anymore. I scream as my fingers open and I tumble down into the ocean.

CHAPTER TEN

I hit the water hard, and the sea quickly swallows me. Churning my arms, I right myself and swim toward a bright patch above me. I break through and gulp air, choking on the salty water that fills my throat.

Through blurred eyes, I see Solitaire Peep leaning over the ship's railing near the bow, waving a flaming torch back and forth over the sea. "Swim to me, boy!" he shouts. I kick hard, heading for the ship.

Gunther's voice rises above the others. "Poor lad will make a fine meal for our finned friends this day!" As his words register, my eyes dart quickly over the water, but it appears as smooth as poured silver.

"They be at port!" Solitaire Peep shouts, sweeping the torch toward the side of the ship. I turn my head; in the fiery orange light of the torch, I see four fins lined up like a row of black sails.

Gasping, I try to swim faster, but the current pushes me away from the ship. My right leg feels odd, as if someone has weighted it with a stone; I cannot will it to move with the rest of my body.

"Swim faster!" Peep screams, waving the burning piece of wood as if a demon possesses him.

"The current!" I gasp, trying to keep my head up. "It's pushing me back." Salt water seeps between my clenched teeth, and I tilt my head higher.

"They're scenting him!" Gunther yells, his voice filled with excitement.

I watch all on the ship's deck turn toward the sharks. Horrified, I see that two have broken away from the others and are gliding toward me.

"Help me!" I scream, pulling hard toward the ship, my injured leg dragging uselessly through the water. I choke as water fills my mouth and nose. My flailing slows as I feel darkness slipping in; a sudden warmth floods through me and brings with it the memory of another day. I see my father standing before the type board in the back of the shop, picking letters from the lower row. I am standing beside him, listening as he teaches me about the importance of keeping the type properly organized. The memory feels wonderful, and I stop struggling in the water, eager for more memories to come.

I slip beneath the surface just as the sea explodes. Geysers of water shoot into the air. Shaken from my dream, I push myself toward the surface. A second firepot explodes beside me, spraying nails and bits of glass. Pain knifes through my shoulder and leg. I feel a fierce tugging on my shirt. I am certain a shark has me. With all the strength I have left, I lash out. My fist connects with flesh.

"Don't fight me, Jameson," the Captain commands in a voice that is low and calm. "We'll both drown if you do." With one arm looped around my chest, he swims with me toward *Destiny*. Exhausted and unable to use my arm or leg, I allow myself to be pulled along. When we reach the ship, Solitaire Peep tosses a grappling hook into the water. The Captain grabs the hook and pulls us toward the ship.

On deck, I kneel, retching up the water I swallowed.

"Aye, spit it out, boy," Solitaire Peep says, pounding me on the back. "You've gulped down half the sea."

Gunther bends low. "We should've left you there," he hisses. "The Captain risked his life and we ours. We wasted precious firepots trying to save your worthless hide."

"Leave him and watch his body be torn to pieces?" The Captain unbuttons his dripping shirt. "I would have done the same for any of my men."

"He brings nothing to this ship but trouble," Gunther says angrily. "Can't even climb down the ratlines properly."

"He wouldn't have fallen had you tied a proper knot." The Captain's voice is hard and accusing. "I could lay this at your feet."

Gunther draws back quickly. His eyes narrow into thin slits. "Surely you don't blame me for the brat's bumbling. I tied a proper knot; could be the boy fiddled with it during the night and loosened it up."

"Perhaps," the Captain says. "That is a question I'll ask Jameson later. Now go summon Cook and tell him to bring needle and thread before I put you in irons for your loose tongue."

"Aye, tell him he'll need a yard of thread this time," Solitaire Peep says, yanking his dagger from its sheath. With a quick flip of his wrist, he slices open my sleeve. "The lad's arm looks like a pincushion and the kicking part of his leg is bent bad."

When Cook sees the blood running down my arm, he clucks his tongue and gets to work quickly. He has brought a bottle of rum up from storage, and he yanks the plug with his teeth and splashes the golden liquid over my shoulder. I gasp as he spreads the skin of my arm apart and places small metal tongs around the head of the nail from the firepot. I feel cold metal against my skin and then fire as he yanks upward, pulling the nail from my wound.

"Give it here," Solitaire Peep says, putting out his hand. "The boy's English blood will mix with the enemy's next time these are used."

The sun is fully risen by the time Cook removes the last nail. I moan as he lifts my arm close to his face and examines it in the sunlight. His hands are slick with blood.

"Are you done?" I whisper.

He shakes his head. "The nails are gone, but I've got to unbury the glass and clay and then stitch you up." He pulls from his pocket the thin-bladed knife he used to pluck the hens. Tiny white feathers and bits of greasy skin cling to the blade. He wipes it quickly across his breeches. "Best I heat the tip to help sear the wound," he says.

Solitaire Peep shakes his head. "We cain't chance a spark will blow into the sails in this wind."

Nodding, Cook splashes more rum on my arm. I yelp as the fire spreads to my shoulder.

"You wouldn't be wailing if we had a cow's tongue to lay across your wounds to lap the pain," Cook says. "At slaughtering time, me mum always saved the cow's tongue for just that reason." He pauses and mops at the trickles of blood that are dripping onto the deck. "Course, if you ain't got a cow's tongue, a wild boar's tongue works second best."

He works slowly, probing with the tip of his knife around each bit of glass or clay until it is loosened and his fingers can grasp it. Every so often, he stops to wipe his fingers on my shirt and then he begins again. From time to time, the pain causes everything to go black, and I let the darkness take me.

When Cook has removed all the glass and clay he can find, he reaches for the threaded needle.

"Clench your teeth, boy," Peep says as he pinches the wound together for Cook to sew. I keep my eyes closed while he stitches me up, moaning softly when the needle jabs through the skin.

When he finishes stitching, Cook turns his attention to my leg. He removes the eyeglass still in my pocket and hands it up to Solitaire Peep. With the tip of his knife, he slices the leg of my breeches up the middle and then rips apart the fabric so that my leg is exposed. He feels along the calf for breaks until he is satisfied there are none. Then he presses in hard with his thumb, stopping just below my knee. "The bone's wiggled out of its holder," he announces. Placing one hand upon my knee and the other hand on the calf, Cook gives a quick twist of his hands, as if he is wringing out a wet rag, and the bone settles into the joint with a loud pop. I feel a sharp pain, and then surprisingly nothing more than a dull ache.

He hobbles to his feet. "The sun will dry out the wounds. Best he stays up on deck for the next few days."

"Take him below," Solitaire Peep says.

"The sun will pull the poison from the wounds faster," Cook argues.

"Maybe, but the Spanish ship hovers like a hawk above a nest. If she attacks, the boy will be in the way." He beckons to Jabbart. "Help Cook take him below. He's no use to us today."

"He's no use to us any day," Gunther mutters as Jabbart and Cook carry me past him to the hatch.

Left alone in storage, I drop into a deep sleep. When I awake, I am unsure of how much time has passed. Night has fallen and has brought with it a full moon that casts deep shadows into the storage room. Rising up from my pallet, I slump against the wall and run my hand lightly over my leg, wincing when I feel around my knee. My arm hangs free from my shirtsleeve, and in the dusky light I see blood oozing from my wounds. I count six stitches and wonder that it's not more. My arm burns as if someone has poured hot pitch over it, and I cannot lift it above my chest.

I think back to the moment I fell into the water, and my

face grows warm with shame. *Can I do nothing right?* Had the Captain not jumped in to save me, I would have drowned or been torn to pieces by the sharks. The Captain risked his life to save me. I close my eyes and am still thinking about that when I lie back on my pallet and drift off to sleep.

༄༺

The clanging of the ship's bell and the sound of steps thudding overhead startle me awake. I lie still for a moment, disoriented in the darkness. Again the bell rings, the noise muted by the ship's thick-planked floors. On the fourth clang, I bolt upright and hold my breath. Three clangs of the bell calls a storm and four warns of a fire or the taking on of water. Five bells signal the approach of an enemy ship.

As the fifth bell sounds, footsteps thud above on deck. My heart begins to pound. "It is only the Spanish ship turning in the water," I murmur. "Nothing to fret about." But an eerie silence has invaded the ship, and I know the crew has taken to their posts. Solitaire Peep has led us in enemy-sighting drills from time to time, and the routine was always the same. It is easy to imagine the scene above my head. The rowers still hold their oars, but their flintlocks and daggers are within reach. The lookouts have abandoned their positions on the ratlines so that they are not the first target for the enemy's pistol. Now they crouch behind barrels, their eyeglasses scanning the moonlit water. Either the Captain or Solitaire Peep is at the tiller, while the other paces the deck giving commands.

I rest my head against the crate. Perhaps the bell had clanged five times in error. Maybe the ringer had lost count. I want to believe that, but in the deepest part of my mind, I know there has been no mistake. The Spanish captain has seen through *Destiny*'s ruse and has turned his ship toward us.

85

With my good arm, I grab hold of a thick rope of onions that dangles from the beam and pull myself up. My clothes are in tatters. My shirtsleeve hangs open off my shoulder and my trousers leg is slit to the ankle. The blood on my clothes has dried dark and crusty, but I give the stains no mind as my hands fumble with a button near the collar. My injured leg feels stiff and sore as I move toward the door, but it holds me up.

Solitaire Peep and the Captain both turn as the hatch squeaks open. Seeing me, the Captain frowns. "You have no place up here."

"I heard the bell clang five times," I say, looking out over the water. My breath catches; the Spanish ship's silhouette looms in the near distance. "Will they attack?"

Solitaire Peep shrugs. "If they are well armed with shot and flint, perhaps. If they are heading to Havana for supplies and their need is great, mayhap they will pass us by."

"When will we know?"

Ferdie, who stands nearby, scoffs at my question. "You'll know when the guns explode. Or do you think they will tie a note to a gull's leg and send it over to us?"

Ignoring him, I ask, "Are we to wait until they fire at us? Surely it would be better to fire first."

The Captain shakes his head. "Haste costs lives. We will bide our time."

With both vessels wary of drawing closer, it is past dawn before the Spanish ship finally moves within clear view of the *Destiny*. Ratty Tom whispers, "There's movement on deck." He raises his eyeglass again, squinting against the sun. "Aye, they're pulling cannons to the edge of the railing."

"A bluff, perhaps," Solitaire Peep says softly. "To let us know they are ready to fight."

"Do they appear ready to strike the flint?" the Captain asks.

"Too many crowd the cannons," Ratty Tom says. "I cannot see clearly."

Gunther snorts. "'Twill be too late when we know for sure."

Ratty Tom looks again. "I count six cannons in front and six more in the back."

Twelve cannons—four more than Destiny carries.

Solitaire Peep snatches the eyeglass from Ratty Tom and places it against his good eye. "Aye, she hugs the water close," he murmurs.

I move beside him. "I don't understand."

Peep passes me the eyeglass. "The ship sits low in the water. No doubt she is heavily armed because she bears treasures for King Philip." He smiles slightly. "Her spoils slow her down. 'Tis unlikely she could give chase and win."

Gunther scowls. "So we are to run instead of fight?"

The Captain hands the tiller off to Ferdie. "We will see her intent before we make our move. If Destiny can get through to Hispaniola without a fight, Queen Anne is better served."

I raise the eyeglass again and position it on the Spanish ship. I see dozens of men scurrying about on the deck. I move the glass to port and see a flurry of movement. Several of the enemy crew have turned to stare at Destiny.

"Call what you see, Jameson," the Captain says.

"They watch us," I whisper. My breath catches as the Spanish captain comes into view. He wears a full uniform sewn in the yellow and garnet colors of the House of Bourbon. Sunlight glints off the silver sword hanging at his side.

"They watch to see if we are loyal to King Philip as our flag declares," Solitaire Peep explains. "When they see our crew wears Queen Anne's colors, they will have their answer."

"Why did we not change?" I ask, thinking of the many crates of clothes below deck, enough to disguise the entire crew.

"The Captain had given the command to do so when you fell," Ferdie says. "'Twas likely witnessed by all. Any fool with an eyeglass would have seen you and the Captain in the water."

"Aye, brat," Gunther says. "You've spoiled it for us."

My face burns. I wait for Peep and the Captain to challenge Gunther's words, but they remain quiet. I open my mouth to defend myself and then close it. There is nothing I can say. Gunther's prediction has come true. I have brought the devil's luck upon them.

I watch in silence as the Spanish captain comes to stand at the railing. Through the eyeglass, I can see his lips moving as he speaks to his crew. Whatever he says causes his men to step away from the cannons, except for the master gunners who maintain their positions. With his eyes fixed upon the *Destiny*, the Spanish captain raises his arm high above his head.

In an instant, I realize his intent. As I turn to cry out a warning, the Spanish captain brings his arm down and the cannons explode.

CHAPTER ELEVEN

The shot from the enemy's cannon slams into the water several feet in front of *Destiny*. The force of the explosion shakes the ship from bow to stern and hurls me backward. Scrambling to my feet, I raise the eyeglass, moving it from side to side until the smoke clears and I can see. "They've turned their cannons toward us!" I shout. "They're loading all of them!"

I am knocked aside as the crew rushes past me to their posts. Jabbart runs to the side cannons and begins helping Gunther shove gunpowder sacks into them.

"Turn!" Solitaire Peep screams, instructing the rowers to move the ship away from the merchant to avoid a direct hit.

The Captain grabs the eyeglass from me. "Help Gunther and Jabbart!"

Gunther tosses me an iron pike. I grab it with both hands, feeling the stitches in my injured arm rip loose as I lift the heavy pike and turn it sideways. "Follow us!" he shouts at me. "Ram it in hard or we'll be blown to bits when I fire the charge!"

I follow behind them, ramming each sack deep into the muzzle with the pike, with no time to wonder if I'm doing it right or to think about the pain that is surging into my shoulder. I stumble back as Gunther lights the charge on the first cannon and flames burst from its mouth. The cannonball tears across the water. Gunther's mark is true, and the metal ball rips through the Spanish merchant's sail. When the smoke clears, all that remains are shreds of canvas.

"Reload!" Gunther shouts as he ignites the next cannon. The second shot misses entirely and hits the water to the left of the Spanish ship's bow. Before Gunther can fire another, the Spanish merchant fires back. Had Peep not given the command to turn the ship away, the ball would have ripped into the side of our vessel. Instead, it hits a corner of the ship's railing near the stern, causing the wood to explode into pieces. The rowers scream and curse as splinters tear into their backs and arms.

"Stay your post and row!" Solitaire Peep yells at the injured men, a few of whom have dropped their oars and look ready to bolt.

Thick clouds of gray smoke rise in wide plumes, making it impossible to see clearly between the two vessels. My lungs feel as if they will burst from breathing in the hot air that is thick with particles of black gunpowder.

"We are moving out of range," Gunther yells to Solitaire Peep. "I cannot hit it from this distance."

"Aye, and they cannot hit us!" Peep calls back. He paces back and forth across the deck.

The words have barely escaped his lips when the Spanish ship fires off two more shots. One falls short, but the other tears into *Destiny*'s mainmast. There is a great cracking sound and then a loud snap. I watch in horror as the top half of the mast slowly leans starboard and then slams into the ocean. The crew runs to the other side of the ship to try to balance the vessel as our ship tilts dangerously toward the water. For a moment, all activity on deck stops as everyone gapes at the chunks of wood and pieces of sail floating in the sea.

"Row out!" the Captain shouts from over his shoulder. He turns the tiller hard to the left, but the loss of the mast and the absence of rowers at their posts have left the ship powerless.

Gunther snatches the pike from me and shoves me aside. He begins moving between the cannons, ramming gunpowder sacks into the heavy guns as if a demon possesses him. He lights one charge and then another, firing shots across the water haphazardly, without any attempt to aim. Not one finds its target. As if satisfied the battle has been won with the destruction of *Destiny's* mainmast, the Spanish merchant begins to pull away.

"Hold fire!" the Captain yells.

"'Twill be death to stop now," Gunther says, panting. "We are at her mercy with a broken mast."

"She has no need to fire upon us," the Captain replies. "We are too damaged to pursue her. She fought only to protect the treasure she carries for Spain."

"We should have destroyed her and taken the treasure," Gunther says. "We waited too long to fire."

"Aye, we might have succeeded with this one, but what if there are others nearby? Ships that carry treasure rarely sail without protection." He raises the eyeglass. "But perhaps this one does. Her rowers are at their post, and she is at full sail. The Spanish captain leaves quickly to avoid another battle."

"And we must do the same," Solitaire Peep says. "We cannot sail farther with a crippled mast." He nods at Jabbart. "Take the boy below to storage and see what can be found to fix it. We'll need a repair that will last four or five days sail from here."

"We'll have to beach for repairs soon," Jabbart says. "I'll need fresh timber to rebuild the mast properly."

"And you shall have it," the Captain says. "Each day the"

winds blow stronger and the air grows cooler. 'Twould be a good time to careen the ship as well." He turns to me. "Your arm needs tending. When you go below, have Cook find bandages and wrap it."

I look down at my arm, surprised to see blood dripping from the wounds. "During the battle, I forgot about the pain."

"That is often the way when it is a fight for life or death. You do not remember what is not important." The Captain pauses. "You fought without complaint and without a child's fear. I am pleased by what I saw."

Peep snorts loudly. "Do not make his head swell so that it will not fit through the hatch. Methinks he could have loaded the guns faster."

"Perhaps," the Captain says. "And he could have stayed below and rightly claimed his injuries, but he did not."

Solitaire Peep's mouth twists, but he nods in agreement.

Gunther throws the pike onto the floor. "Had the brat not given us away, we would not be retreating." He stares hard at me. "And why would he show a child's fear if he is sixteen as he claims?"

My heart begins to pound. My age has not been mentioned since the first day on the ship. Now the words stick in my throat.

The Captain laughs. "It is not age alone that determines a man. I have seen grown men hide when the fighting began."

Peep cuts in. "Aye, remember the fool we took on four summers ago after we left Panama? He was white in the hair, but he shivered at the talk of battle."

My head shot up. "Where is this man now?"

Ferdie snorts. "His bones float from here to Port Royal," he says. "A terrible storm blew in one night. The sea washed over the railing and claimed the poor oaf."

"Aye," Gunther says. "He couldn't even tack down a sail the right way. 'Twas our luck a storm blew up and carried him away."

"You have made that remark often, Gunther," the Captain says in a voice that holds questions. "I still do not know why the man was up on deck when I had given orders for everyone to go below."

Gunther shrugs. "He was a fool the day he came aboard, and stayed a fool 'til the sea took him. It's like I told the brat—accidents are commonplace on a sailing ship."

I draw a sharp breath. There is no mistaking Gunther's meaning. I glance at the Captain, but he and Solitaire Peep have turned their attention to Ratty Tom, who is scurrying up the battered lines to survey the damage to the mast. My eyes meet Gunther's. "Too bad for him," I say. "But the same will not happen to me."

Gunther leans close until his breath blows hot into my face. "'Twill if I say so," he whispers.

Sensing trouble, Solitaire Peep turns toward us. "What are you saying to the lad, Gunther?" he asks, "What is so important that you neglect the guns?"

Gunther hawks loudly and spits a thick gray glob over the busted railing. "I was telling him to push the pike in a bit harder next time. Teaching him like his poor dead papa would have."

My face flames in anger. "You soil my father's memory by mention of him."

Gunther swipes his hand over his mouth and grins. Before he can reply, Solitaire Peep steps between us. He places his hand on my back, pressing hard with bony fingers to silence me. "Do as the Captain said; go below and tend your wounds."

With Cook's help, I bandage my arm. Then, I join with two others who are helping Jabbart fashion a makeshift mast out of two beams he has pulled down from the ceiling of the storage room. We saw and hack at the solid oak beam until Jabbart is satisfied that the thickness is right. Finally, Jabbart declares the task to be finished. "'Tis as good as we can make it for now," he says.

I stand and brush the sawdust from my hands. "Will it take us to where we will beach?"

"Aye, unless we do battle again." Jabbart grabs one end of the beam. "Take the other," he says to us. "'Twill be hard to get this up with night winds, but get it up we must."

It takes most of the crew to hoist the new beam up to the broken mast. I stand beneath the lines and help feed it up to the ratmen as they climb the lines. Strong gusts push the beam from side to side, and the men struggle to maintain their grip. At the top, they secure the new mast to what is left of the old with several yards of thick hemp roping, tying knots atop one another until it stands upright.

When the sails are once again full, Peep sends me below to the Captain's cabin. "Ask him for the Yellow Jack," he says.

I find the Captain standing before his mirror, shaving. Turning slightly, he nods toward his desk. "What you have come for is on my desk."

I pick up the plain yellow flag and run my hand over the smooth silk. "Do you plan another ruse?" I ask, thinking yellow is one of King Philip's colors.

The Captain wipes his mouth and drops the soiled rag next to his razor cup. "When the other ships see we fly the Yellow Jack, they will not come near. We are assured a safe journey."

"No disrespect intended, sir, but you said the same when we raised King Philip's flag."

"Aye, but this is different," the Captain says. "I raised the

Spanish flag so that we could sail into Spanish territory. But now that we sail away, the Yellow Jack will serve our purpose well." He sits behind his desk. "Do you remember when the plague came to Charles Towne last spring…how your neighbors reacted when the boils appeared?"

"Yes sir. I remember clearly. My father went to the neighbor's wife and begged her to come and help tend my mother."

"Did she?"

I shake my head. When I speak, I cannot keep the bitterness from my tone. "She turned my father away at her door and would not let him enter."

"And rightly so," the Captain says, "for plagues are passed from hand to hand, breath to breath." He holds out his hand, and I place the flag in it. With a snap of his wrist, the Captain unfurls the bright yellow flag. "This banner tells all who see it that yellow fever has taken hold of the ship. It is a powerful warning to stay away."

My eyes widen. "Who has fallen sick?"

"No one. You miss the point. This flag guarantees that we will sail unmolested out of Spanish waters. It ensures our safety."

"How is that, sir?" I ask.

The Captain smiles. "When the enemy sees the Yellow Jack unfurled above the *Destiny*, they will turn their ships away and pray for full sails. Now take the flag to Peep and then get some sleep. Come morning, you are to resume your sketching; we are still in Spanish waters and there is much to record."

The next morning, I begin my sea-artist duties as soon as I come up on deck. While we move through the water, I record the ship's position on my compass and then write it on the parchment. At midday, Cook brings the goat up on deck and lets her roam free. Her bleating breaks the silence, and I stop and pat her on the head when she comes near.

I have cut the other sleeve from my shirt, leaving both arms bare to the sun. The heat feels good against my wounds and already scabs are beginning to form. During our first weeks at sea, the sun burned and peeled my skin, but in time the redness disappeared, leaving my arms the color of faded walnuts. Now, my arms are streaked with dirt and specks of gunpowder. *I'll bathe tonight*, I think, remembering an extra uniform in one of the crates; perhaps the Captain will allow me to wear it. I feel a pang of guilt at the thought. I have no desire to be a sailor for long. But as each day passes, returning to Charles Towne seems more and more unlikely. Looking up, I squint into the sun. "I shall be a printer some day," I murmur to myself. "I will not forget my father's trade." Having said the words aloud, I feel better. I resolve that later I will ask the Captain if I can wear the Queen's colors. I sail on her ship and I risk my life to defend it. Why shouldn't I wear a proper uniform?

That night, Cook serves a supper that sets the crew to grumbling. Steam rises from the cauldron and wafts over to where I sit taking apart a barrel that is black with rot. When I have tied together the good pieces that can be reused, I brush the wood dust from my trousers and go to eat. I peer over Cook's shoulder into his pot. The eyeballs looking back at me cause me to recoil. Floating on top of a thick gray broth is a monstrous creature with two milky eyes that bulge from the top of its head. Surrounding its head are many legs that curl around each other and float atop the liquid. I grimace and swallow hard to push down the bile that has filled my throat.

Cook scowls when he sees my face. "Don't turn up your nose at my stew," he says, "for 'tis as good a meal as you're likely to get until we beach. Lucky for us, the poor thing got tangled in me net this morning." He reaches into the pot and hacks off a portion of one of the creature's legs and scoops it into my bowl.

I consider dumping the bowl over the railing when Cook isn't looking, but he watches me, eyes narrowed. I spear the leg with my fork and bite into it. Satisfied, Cook turns back to his cauldron.

The meat is so chewy, I'm afraid to swallow for fear I might choke. I chew and chew, and then finally, I swallow hard and follow it up with a long swig of ale. The taste in my mouth is sour and fishy, and I hold my breath until I have eaten it all.

After supper, I fill Cook's scalding tub with seawater for my bath. I no longer feel shy about stripping in front of the others. On a ship the size of *Destiny*, privacy is impossible. I pull off my shirt and am standing in my breeches when the Captain appears.

"A bath feels good after a day's battle," he says. "You have earned the right to a soak."

I nod, wondering how to ask for the uniform. Taking a deep breath, I say, "Sir, there is a crate below that holds two uniforms of the Royal Navy. I thought…I thought perhaps…" Suddenly, asking seems impudent. I am a boy from Charles Towne, not a royal sailor.

"You thought what, Jameson?"

I raise my head. "I thought I might wear one, that is, until you take on new men and need it back."

The Captain rubs his chin. "The uniform you speak of is to be worn only by those who serve Queen Anne gladly—those who will risk their lives for her good."

"It is true that I did not want to serve at first," I say. "But I have done as commanded."

"I can see that your heart remains in Charles Towne," the

Captain says. "You would return tomorrow given the chance. Isn't that also true?"

I shake my head. "I will return only when I can follow my father's trade...when I can return as a free man and not as a servant to a baker."

"So the baker's trade is no longer fit for you?" he asks. "Three months at sea and you have forgotten the debt you owe?"

"I've forgotten nothing," I say. "But lately I have thought about that day in the bakery. I was starving, but I never would have left the shop with the bread. The baker took advantage of me."

"How so?" the Captain asks.

"It makes no sense that the baker would purchase the term of the thief who stole from him. Did he not worry that I would steal his coins when his head was turned?"

"Perhaps he thought to redeem you."

"No," I say, scowling. "The baker accused me falsely and then saw an opportunity to purchase my term cheaply at the auction. He is of low character, for sure."

The Captain smiles. "You will do well in this world, Jameson. You do not look for the bad that exists, but you recognize it when you see it. Life often sends us hard lessons, but you have learned this one well. It is not likely you will be caught off guard again."

A breeze blows across the deck and gently ripples the water in the tub. I pick up my shirt from the deck and move it away from the tub so that it will not get wet. "Tell Peep to issue you a uniform," the Captain says. "You fought like a loyal subject this morning, Jameson. You have earned the right to wear Her Majesty's colors."

I lift my chin. "I will wear Queen Anne's colors and fight for her good. But I must tell you honestly that someday I will follow in my father's steps and put the skills he taught me to good use."

"Aye, Jameson. Someday, but not too soon. *Destiny* needs a sea artist."

"Then I shall serve as one until the time comes that I can go safely home to Charles Towne." With those words, I grab my tattered shirt from the deck and fling it over the railing, smiling as the shirt floats slowly away.

CHAPTER TWELVE

After my bath, I go below to feed and water the animals. Then I pull on the clean sleeping shirt that Cook gave me from one of the crates. The pain that shoots through my arm as I dress reminds me that much has changed since the sun rose in the morning sky.

The sleeves of the nightshirt are long, with cuffs that have two rows of silver stitching sewn in loops around the edge. The soft ivory cloth feels cold against my skin. I rub my finger gently over the threads. Cook told me that the shirt came from the Orient where magical worms weave the fabric day and night. He said 'twas likely I would find myself curled up like a grub in the morning if I wore it to bed.

For the first time since leaving Charles Towne, I am excited for morning to come. Solitaire Peep wouldn't tell me a lot about the island to which we sail, only that it is crossed, much like the St. George's Cross that adorns Her Majesty's flag. Jabbart said he hoped it was the same island they had sailed to several seasons ago, as the trees were plentiful and he would be sure to find what he needed for the new mast.

The ship dips hard tonight, and I can hear the waves beating into its sides. Cook says that the lack of stars in the sky means that come morning, we will be in the midst of a battle between the gods of the sea and wind. He claims a starless night means the gods have all taken cover so they will not be pulled down from the heavens or washed away by the sea. Already the ship rocks, and each dip causes my stomach to roll. I lie back down and try to settle in, but the pains are so sharp that they force me up a few minutes later. Holding my stomach, I belch loudly several times, but the ache does not subside. The spasms spread from my naval to my ribs, and each throb flushes my body with heat. The goat nudges me, bleating softly. I shake my head and gently push her away. "It was that awful sea creature," I mutter, wondering why Cook didn't toss it back into the sea. The storage room is filled with food; eating such a beast makes no sense. I curl up on my mat and hope the pain will pass so I do not have to go in search of the night bucket. Instead the throbbing grows worse. Finally, I throw off my sheet. Morning is hours away, and I cannot wait.

The ship tilts abruptly and I stumble down the unlit hall, pressing my palms against the wall for support. The ship heaves and lurches as if in a game of tug-of-war. The night bucket is nowhere to be found, so I am forced to go up on deck.

A chilly blast of wet air envelopes me as I ease open the hatch. Rain cascades across the deck, and I regret that I did not wrap a tarp around myself before coming up. I glance uneasily toward the back of the ship, my eyes finding the flat board that hangs beyond the railing, high above the water. A round hole has been cut in the middle of the board. I have seen others use the contraption, but I have never dared try, preferring the bucket instead. The thought of balancing upon a board that dangles over the sea terrifies me. Tonight though, I have no choice; the bucket is not in its usual place, and I cannot wait a minute longer.

Jabbart, on lookout near the cannons, shakes his head when he sees my predicament. "You're not the only one sick from Cook's feast," he says. "Half the ship has been up here since supper."

I double over as another spasm hits. "The creature squeezes my gut something awful."

"There are rags beneath the steps," Jabbart says. "Take a few and leave some for the others. I will have more company this night, I'm sure."

Climbing atop the board turns out to be easier than I imagined. Two crates serve as steps, and I need only to reach out and grab the ropes to bring the board to me so that I can climb atop. Staying seated, however, proves more difficult. The heavy wind causes the board to swing from side to side. More than once I must push away from the railing so that I do not bang into the ship's side, all the while hoping that I don't fall into the sea. A steady rain beats upon my back as I clutch the ropes, and I try not to think of the churning water below me and the sharks that I saw earlier.

When I drop back onto the deck a few minutes later, I say to Jabbart, "I will starve before I eat anything with legs from this sea again."

Jabbart sighs, his eyes upon the water, "'Twould surprise you what you might eat if you're starving," he says. "I've seen men boil boot leather to fill their bellies."

I remember the hunger I felt after being turned out of my father's shop. For days I wandered through Charles Towne's streets without a shilling to buy a rotting apple. I recall how good the fish stew tasted on my first day aboard ship. For the few minutes I spent eating that meal, I forgot my fears. The Captain's words about hunger come back to me and I repeat them to Jabbart.

"Aye," he agrees as I lift the hatch to go below. "Hunger is indeed a powerful master."

The hall seems darker as I make my way back below deck;

not a speck of light filters through the planking. When I open the door to the storage room, the goat bleats loudly. "Quiet," I whisper. "If you wake Peep, 'twill be my skin he takes." She cries louder still, and I reach out to rub her side.

"What's this?" I murmur when I feel her wet fur. "How did you get soaked?" Too tired to worry, I sink down onto my pallet, only to bolt up again when I feel water seeping through my clothing. Patting the floor with my palms, I follow the water to where the floorboard meets the side of the ship. Water spurts through the seams. Large puddles have pooled beneath the hens' crates. *This is bad*, I think, hurrying toward the door. Whatever caused the leak must be fixed—and quick.

Solitaire Peep's hammock swings next to Cook's in a narrow room off the galley. Both men lie sleeping beneath a tightly woven fishing net that shields them from the flies and mosquitoes that terrorize the ship at night.

I give Solitaire Peep a shake. "Wake up! There's a leak in the storage room!"

Peep's head is tilted back and his breath comes in loud drawn-out snorts.

"Wake up!" I shout again.

He springs up wide-eyed and grabs my wrist. "What are you doing to me whilst I sleep?" he snarls.

I try to wrench my arm away, but Solitaire Peep holds fast and pulls me closer. "Did you think to steal my patch?"

"For what reason?" I ask, turning my face from Peep's breath, which is fouled by the creature he ate earlier.

"Lucky for you I can think of no answer," Peep says, releasing me. "Why then do you wake me from my sleep?"

I rub my wrist. "The storage room leaks. Already the animals' crates are soaked and puddles run along the sides."

"Does it leak from the ceiling?"

I shake my head. "On the floor where the barrels are stacked."

Adjusting his eye patch, Solitaire Peep swings out of the hammock. "Wake Cook and have him heat some tar. The crack will need sealing."

⚘

Cook and I are in the galley stirring a small cauldron of bubbling hot tar when we hear Solitaire Peep yell. We leave the cauldron and hurry to the storage room. I freeze in the doorway. Water sprays out like a fountain from the side of the wall. The floor is flooded. "Clang the bell, lad," Solitaire Peep shouts. "We're taking on water!"

"I'll heat more pitch," Cook says, hobbling back toward the galley.

Up on deck, I grab the gong and slam it twice against the bell.

Jabbart raises his head in alarm. "Where's it coming in?"

"Storage," I say, pausing to catch my breath. "Water is shooting through the sides." From below I can hear the Captain rousing the crew from their sleep. When I return to the storage room, the men have gathered. Cook and Peep are on their knees packing the leaking crevices with strips of hemp and steaming hot tar. It seems as if the ship's entire side has split open. Whenever they seal a spot, a new gush of water erupts nearby. The smoke from the pitch burns my eyes and fills my lungs.

"Tell Jabbart to get down here," the Captain snaps. "We need a carpenter to repair this leak, not a cook." He motions to Ferdie. "Go up and take over as lookout."

Startled by the commotion around them, the hens cackle loudly and flap their wings hard, sending white feathers into the air. I grab their crates and carry them into the hall.

A few minutes later, Jabbart shoves past me and goes to where Cook and Peep still work at sealing the leaks. Kneeling down, he runs his hands along the side, shoving his fingers into the crevice to determine the damage. After a few moments, he stands and wipes his hands on his pants. "We can't properly fix a hole this size while we're under sail," he says. "We can plug it now, but these boards will need to be replaced when she is careened on the island."

"What has caused this?" the Captain asks.

Jabbart shrugs. "Could be the new mast is unbalanced and is putting too much pressure on this side of the ship. Mayhap we hit something beneath the water that ripped a hole in the outer plankings. Can't say whilst she's in the water."

"We're five days sail to a safe beach. Can she make it?"

Jabbart hesitates before speaking. "If we lighten her load and the weather's good, mayhap we can."

"How much weight can she take?"

"The crew and the guns and a couple of barrels of food, but not much more than that," Jabbart says. "She needs to sit higher in the water."

I draw a deep breath and survey the crates and barrels in the room, most still full of food.

The Captain turns to Cook. "Keep a barrel of meat, a sack of flour, all the cheese and salt, some ale, and the tea. Everything else goes into the water."

His words draw a gasp from me and others in the room. A low murmuring begins.

"You cain't mean to throw out our food," Gunther objects.

"We have no choice," the Captain responds. "We toss it or risk sinking."

"We can turn back and sail to a closer beach," Ferdie says.

Solitaire Peep snorts. "Beach in Spanish waters? The enemy will sneak up on us whilst the ship's careened."

The Captain holds up his hand and the room grows quiet.

"Where we head is a week's sail from Charles Towne. Once the ship is repaired, we'll sail back there and refill the hold."

The Captain's words startle me. *Sail to Charles Towne*. A few days ago I would have been thrilled to hear such news. But now... Things are different. I need time to think about what going back to Charles Towne would mean. The thinking will have to wait, though. Solitaire Peep shouts at us to get moving. I grab a sack of barley near my feet and drag it down the hall and up to the deck. I throw it over the side and head back to the storage room. There is little talk amongst the crew, but I hear much grumbling as we toss overboard dozens of sacks of barley and flour, two barrels of dried red beans, three kegs of dried beef, and all the other food that was taken on back in Charles Towne. Cook stands guard beside the barrel of salted beef, a sack of flour, the cheese wheels, and the half-dozen small kegs of ale he has been allowed to keep. When the last sack of barley hits the water, I grip the railing and stare out over the sea. The moon's bright light upon the black water taunts me as I watch *Destiny*'s food supply disappear beneath the waves. My thoughts turn back to the morning when I awoke in the alley and saw the yellow-striped cat nibbling a shiny sliver of pig fat. The hollowness in my stomach had driven me to try to snatch the fat from the cat's claws. I hoped never to feel such hunger again.

Disheartened, I return to the storage room. A gray haze from the hot pitch fills the room. The hens wander about freely, their crates having been tossed overboard with the rest of the supplies. My pallet has been kicked to the side of the room, and cornhusks poke through holes made when it was trampled. I bite my lip as I look around the room, which has become a home to me in the weeks since my capture, a place where I can shut the door at night and sleep or call back the memories of my life before the plague. Now it looks as if the

Queen's army has galloped through. I gather up the straw that was dumped out of the hen's crates and form a mound in a dry corner for them to nest in. Old sails that were used to mop the water lie all around. They are heavy, but I manage to drag them into a sodden heap by the door. Tomorrow, I will hang them over the railing to dry.

As I work, I think about what lies ahead. Without the barrels and sacks, there is more space in the room for the animals to roam. I can help Cook net fish every day, and that will help make our food supplies last longer. Though the Captain has said he will refill the hold as soon as *Destiny* has been repaired, something gnaws at me, a feeling of unease that won't go away. *That is because it's night*, I think. *Everything appears worse in the dark.* Tomorrow, when the sun glistens on the deck and *Destiny* sails toward English waters, I will feel better.

Yawning loudly, I find a dry sail atop a barrel. I fold it several times and place it over my wet pallet. I close my eyes and try to sleep, but images of water pouring through the sides and barrels of food being tossed into the dark sea fill my head. Though the room is stifling hot, a chill runs through me, and I shiver. A long while passes before I finally drift off.

CHAPTER THIRTEEN

The storm leaves behind strong winds that fill our sails for the next three days. Solitaire Peep is pleased, for the crew is relieved from rowing, and they do not grumble so much over the half rations the Captain has ordered. Though we are still in Spanish waters, the sea has changed from a blue as bright as a robin's egg to a brown deeper than brewed tea. Peep says that as we sail closer to La Florida, the water will begin to look like new spring grass. On the parchment, I make note of such things, for Peep says changes in the sea's color are almost as useful as the markings of a map.

Yesterday, Ratty Tom called a Spanish ship on the horizon. By the Captain's orders we stood ready, our pistols filled with shot and our daggers sharpened. Gunther moved the cannons into place, and Peep ordered the firepots uncovered, but the enemy suddenly turned and sailed quickly away. He said that the sun's glint off the Yellow Jack is a powerful warning; even those who are tempted to fire upon the Queen's ship will not sail near.

I have worn my new uniform since the morning after the storm. When I came through the hatch that first day, some of the crew looked my way, but no one said anything, not even Gunther. The jacket's sleeves are long, so I fold the material back at the wrist so I don't stain it with ink when I sketch. The pants droop low at the waist, but I have tied them with a length of rigging, and they stay up well enough.

The Captain seems pleased with my work. I have used the compass as he showed me, filling almost two whole sheets of parchment with small drawings that one day can be copied into a whole map. Sometimes, I sketch pictures of the ocean and place in the middle a tall wave upon which sits a ship with two masts and billowing sails. I long for colored ink to capture the shades of the sea. Lately, I have wished for a bottle of white ink, too, so that I could add a drop to make the gray wings of the gulls that are now common overhead. They bring to mind the birds that stand one-legged on the posts in Charles Towne's harbor; they watch the ships arriving, their heads turning ever so slightly as if they are soldiers guarding the town. Though my heart longs to return, the thought fills my belly with fear. I am a posted runaway. The best I can hope for is a lashing, but men have been hanged for less.

Today, I must wait to begin my sketching. It takes me most of the morning to clean up after the animals. Fresh straw is now scarce, so I sort the clean pieces from those that are clumped together with pig dung, onion skins that have floated from the rafters, and dead flies. The goat does not stray from my side as I work. She follows me about the room, rubbing her head against my sleeve and snorting. The garment smells of the cloves and mint that Cook packed around it to ward off the moths, and I think our little goat is reminded of a field that she once roamed.

I am further distracted from my duties this morning by the growling beast inside my stomach. I vow to save something from my supper tonight, no matter how much I want to eat it. We are on half rations now by the Captain's orders; breakfast today was three biscuits and a bit of cheese that was tainted with mold, but not enough to spoil the taste. Yesterday, Cook's net came up empty except for a few crabs and two fish with long black whiskers that sprung from each side of the mouth. He says the storm scared the fish away from the surface. The stew he boiled from the whiskered fish tasted good, but too many small bones floated in my bowl. I feared choking every time I swallowed.

I am concentrating on drawing a straight line that does not go jaggedly into another when Ratty Tom cries out, "Land ahead! Land straight ahead!"

My eyes widen when I lift my head. An island looms before us, a jagged mass that reminds me of the way spilled ink spreads on a sheet of parchment. One corner of the island stretches east and the other west. A strong wind propels *Destiny* toward the middle, and I hear Peep command the rowers to take to their benches so they can control the ship as she heads toward the island.

I long to stand over the railing as we draw closer, but instead I begin to outline the shape of the island. Suddenly Solitaire Peep is at my side. "Put the paper away, boy," he says. "There's no need to draw Crossed Island."

I look at him curiously. "The Captain said I should sketch everything I see."

"Aye, but not the island," Peep insists. "'Tis too risky."

"Why?" I ask absentmindedly, studying the compass.

"Didn't you hear me?" Peep snaps. Bending down, he covers the compass with his hand so that I cannot record the island's location. "Stop your marking!"

Sighing, I lay down the quill. "Fine by me," I say, glad for an excuse to go stand by the railing. It is easy to understand how the island got its name; from a distance, it looks like a cross lying flat against the ground.

"You said sketching was too risky. What did you mean?" I ask.

Peep moves closer and whispers, "We cain't risk your recordings falling into the hands of our enemies."

I laugh and wave my arm over the rail. "Our enemies would be blind not to glimpse the island from the sea. It is as wide as Charles Towne's harbor."

"Aye, they can no doubt see it," Solitaire Peep replies, smiling. "But why would they venture to beach here? There is nothing of use except timber to repair a ship, and there are other islands closer to Spanish ports if that is what they desire. Put a mark upon my word, the enemy ships may pass by, but they will not stay long."

I look at Peep in dismay. If the enemy spotted us here, crippled with a broken mast, wouldn't we be in terrible danger?

He claps his hand down on my shoulder and laughs, as if he can read my mind. "When we've rowed ashore, step lively through the sand, lest the scorpions have time to nibble on your flesh."

I leave the railing and begin packing away my kit and rolling up the parchment. "Will we go ashore today, then?"

Peep nods. "Aye, before the stars twinkle, we'll be on Crossed Island." He breathes deeply and I can see that he is pleased. "It has been a long time, but I've forgotten nothing," he adds.

I snort. "What is there to forget about such a place?"

Solitaire Peep turns away. "Your nose is too long, boy," he says. "You ask too many questions." Halfway to the hatch, he turns back. "Remember what I said. Keep the island's markings in your noggin and off the paper."

Though forbidden to sketch, I remain on deck, filling the hours with one chore after another. The oarsmen's benches stay full, so I polish the ship's railing with whale fat, and then wash down the deck, looking for any chore that will give me a reason to stay up on deck.

Other than climb the rigging, something I haven't tried again since my fall, I've learned most of the duties of a royal sailor. I have become what Solitaire Peep refers to as the "all-around," filling in wherever an extra hand is needed. Most of the time, though, I sketch. And when the oarsmen look my way and smirk as if I am a child at play, I remind myself that my father served in a trade that often went unnoticed, but that did not make it less valuable than others.

☙ ❧

As Solitaire Peep predicted, the Captain gives the order to lay anchor when the first stars appear in the sky. *Destiny's* huge iron anchor requires three men to lift it over the side. A loud cheer sounds when the anchor hits the water with a resounding splash, and the longboats are immediately lowered.

Cook brings out a handful of straw and the crew gathers around to draw lots; those who pull out the longest stalks will be in the first boats rowed to shore. I sigh, disappointed, when I hold up my straw beside the rest. I wanted to row ashore with the Captain.

Seeing my face, Jabbart laughs and ruffles my hair. "Don't fret; you'll feel the earth beneath your feet soon enough," he says.

I shrug. At least I won't be in the same boat as Gunther and Ferdie, who have each drawn a long straw.

Those who remain on board try to keep busy, but their eyes wander across the black water. I absentmindedly cut frays from the piles of hemp roping and then retie the ends, impatiently waiting for Peep to give the command to lower another boat.

As the hour passes, there is much speculation about what the island might be like, and I realize that no one in the present crew except the Captain, Solitaire Peep, and Cook has ever been there. An excited murmur sweeps the deck when a flash of orange appears suddenly across the water. Cook has found a dry spot to light a fire. Before leaving the ship, the Captain ordered supper to be served only when the entire crew has gathered on the beach. Cook, who left in the first boat, carried with him a bag of flour for the evening biscuits as well as a slab of cheese wrapped in cloth, a kettle, and a sackful of trenchers.

Solitaire Peep orders the last boat filled and finally it is my turn. A deep darkness spreads over the water, making it impossible to see anything except the orange glow from the beach. I start carefully down the rope ladder. We have all been instructed to take our sleep pallets and though I have rolled mine and tied it tightly with rope, it weighs awkwardly in my hands as I climb into the longboat.

Peep unknots the lines hat secure the longboat to *Destiny*, and then takes his place near the hull. "Push off," he commands.

Using the end of my oar, I help to push away from *Destiny*. The longboat tilts sharply and cold water washes over the side, soaking us all. Muttering a curse, Solitaire Peep orders two of the men to move to the other side for balance. After careful maneuvering, the boat heads toward land.

The incoming tide carries the vessel quickly toward the beach. I grip my oar firmly and pull it through the waves. Water sprays up from the sides as the crew finds their rhythm and guides the narrow vessel toward land.

As the boat nears the island, the smell of decaying plants and muddy earth fills the air. A shrill cry comes suddenly out of the darkness, a pleading sound that causes the hair on my neck to rise. I grip the oar harder, my eyes searching through the thick blackness of the distant trees. The cry comes again, loud and angry.

"'Tis human," I whisper.

"Nay," Solitaire Peep replies. "'Tis only the swamp owls calling our arrival."

"To whom?" I ask, alarmed.

"To the other creatures that live on the island, that's who," says Solitaire Peep. "The forests are thick with wild birds and the like."

My eyes settle on Cook's fire. Flames lick the air, setting embers adrift in the black sky. It occurs to me that such a large fire is not necessary to brown the supper biscuits. "Cook's fire will surely attract the enemy," I say to Peep. "Why does he risk such a large one?"

"To keep the wild animals away," Peep replies. "A fire must burn each night or we'll all awake to find our legs being carted off by the wild pigs that roam the forest. Besides, from a distance, the enemy will not be able to tell if it's a fire that burns or if it is the moon shining upon the water."

Through the orange glow, I glimpse the crew huddled around the fire. I notice immediately that the Captain isn't among them. Before I can sort that out, the boat hits hard into a sandbar. "Get out, boy," Peep commands, "and help bring the boat onto the beach."

Removing my boots, I lay down my oar and leap over the side along with Ratty Tom. The water, still warm from the day's sun, laps at my waist. We jerk the rope and pull the boat toward the shore. The others still in the boat lean over the sides and push their oars along the shallow bottom to move it along. I stumble twice as my feet sink into the sand, but I catch myself before the boat can overrun me. At the beach, the others jump out and help us drag the boat high onto the sand.

Solitaire Peep points to a thick line of trees. "We'll tie it to the stump over there," he says.

I loop the rope over my shoulder and we pull the boat toward the stump. Solitaire Peep comes up behind me. "Tie it right or come morning 'twill be gone with the outgoing tide. Weave the rope through the loop," he says, pointing toward the stump's base.

When I look down, I see a gold ring protruding from the stump. I kneel in the sand and run my hand over the ring, discovering that it's not a ring at all, but rather a piece of pewter twisted into a half circle. Someone has embedded the twisted ends deep into the tree. There is no need for me to ask who has done so; of all the trees and stumps along the shoreline, Solitaire Peep had known exactly which one to head for.

As I thread the rope through the ring, I think about the island. From a distance, it seems like nothing special. But a question nags at me: with a broken mast and the daily threat of storms that could sink us, why had the Captain risked sailing to Crossed Island? Surely, we could have charted course to a closer island. Troubled, I give the rope a final tug and hurry back toward the fire, where the others have gathered to eat.

After ladling broth into the trenchers, Cook tosses dried grass into the fire. With each handful, the flames crackle loudly and roar toward the night sky. I ease in beside Jabbart. Despite the fire, the air holds a chill. My shirt and pants are soaked from wading through the surf, and they will likely stay that way until the next day's sun dries them. Others have brought along some of their belongings, and I feel a pang of regret that I did not think to do the same. Now I will have to sleep in wet clothes.

I stir my soup, turning over a root of some sort, its leaves still attached. Other than that, there is nothing in the broth except for a few morsels of fish. I bite into one biscuit, pocketing the other to eat when the others sleep and I cannot. Lately my nights have been plagued with thoughts of home. In my mind's eye, I see the two-story house and remember how it leans toward the street. I chew my biscuit slowly until it dissolves and there is no danger that it will lodge against the lump that fills my throat.

A few of the men drift from the fire to spread their pallets on the sand. I wonder who will stand guard for the night. It is unlikely Peep will fail to post a lookout, as if no harm can come to us here.

I glance up and down the beach, searching for the Captain, who did not appear for supper. My eyes fall upon the thicket of trees that line the edge of the beach. Their leaves glisten silvery-green beneath the moon's hazy light. Surely the Captain would not remain in the forest at this late hour.

Suddenly, the swamp owl I had heard earlier screams again, its piercing cry rising and falling until I place my hands over my ears to block out the sound. It occurs to me that only the owl knows if the Captain has gone beyond the trees, for no human eyes could see through such darkness. Is that what the owl is saying? Is it calling out to other creatures that the Captain has trespassed amongst them?

The crew begins to settle in for the night, arranging their sleeping mats around the fire. My eyelids are heavy, so I find a clear space and unroll my pallet. I close my eyes and will myself to sleep. When morning comes, there will be much to do and consider. Now, in the darkness, there are no answers to be had.

CHAPTER FOURTEEN

I wake near dawn to a swarm of mosquitoes buzzing loudly near my head. My face feels as if it is on fire, the skin hot and swollen. "This place is not fit for animals," I mutter.

Swatting at mosquitoes clinging to my shirt, I pull my pallet over beside Jabbart's and Ratty Tom's. Their even snores tell me they have not suffered the same fate. I scratch a welt on my neck, vowing to sleep closer to the fire from now on.

The salt from the water has left my clothing stiff. I tug on my trouser legs as I walk to the stump where I tied the boat the night before. I give two quick yanks on the rope and then drop it, satisfied the vessel is still secure. The others are just waking, and so I walk down the beach, enjoying the feel of the white sand beneath my feet and the sun on my face. In the morning light, the island doesn't seem as hostile as it did the night before.

I eye the trees that line the edge of the beach like soldiers blocking entry into the thick woods that lie behind them. Two tall oaks, their trunks charred black by lightning, stand side by side. The narrow gap between them looks like a doorway into the woods. Around the base of both trees grows a thick green vine covered with red berries. I squat for a closer look, remembering the berries that grew wild each summer behind the print shop, and the way my mother picked them to make jam and pies. With food supplies low, perhaps Cook can put these berries to good use.

Holding up the bottom of my shirt to use as a basket, I pull the brightest ones from the vine. When only hard green ones are left, I step between the charred oaks in search of more.

The forest is cool and dark inside, shielded by thick branches that form a wide canopy across the sky and block out the light. Pine needles, dry palms, and clumps of gray moss blanket the ground. I breathe deeply, inhaling air tinged with pine.

The quietness of the woods causes me to forget about Solitaire Peep's warning and the cries from the animals I heard the night before. I concentrate on picking the berries, imagining how pleased Cook will be when I return with them. The vine seems endless as I follow it farther into the woods.

When my shirt can hold no more, I turn to leave. I am almost at the charred oaks when I hear a loud rustling of leaves that causes me to spin around. A large black boar, his snout to the ground, appears suddenly from beneath a bush. The boar seems as startled to see me as I am to see him. He stares at me with closely set eyes that look to be crossed.

I draw a sharp breath. The boar's tusks are as sharp as any dagger I have ever seen, capable of cutting me to the bone. With my eyes on the animal, I edge slowly backwards. Alarmed at my movement, the boar's ears flicker. He raises his head and snorts loudly.

"Easy," I whisper.

The boar's lips curl back over rows of pointed yellow teeth. When he begins pawing at the ground with his hoof, I know he has no intention of letting me escape. I drop the berries and grab for the dagger hanging at my side. Instantly the boar springs at me, teeth bared and snarling. His tusk catches me below the knee, knocking me backwards. I stumble, but I manage to stay on my feet. I yank my knife free and crouch, ready in case the boar turns and charges again. When he does, I step quickly to the side and stab wildly at him with my dagger, plunging it deep into the flesh near the back of his neck. The sight of blood spurting upward shocks me, and I stumble back. The boar falls, rises to his feet, staggers toward me, and then collapses. I wait with my knife raised, but he doesn't move again.

I sink back against a tree, my heart pounding. Blood spills down my leg. Ripping a piece of fabric from my torn pants, I wrap it tightly around the wound. My leg hurts, but the pain is worth it. The boar is large and will feed us for many nights.

I limp slowly back toward camp, dragging the carcass awkwardly behind me. Cook's eyes widen when he sees what I have brought. "Has the man in the moon stolen your wits, boy?" he asks. "One who hunts the wild pig with only a knife is surely asking to die."

"It was more like he hunted me," I reply. "He attacked me whilst I was in the woods."

"Lucky for you the moon was full last night," Cook says. "Animals with tusks are weakened after a full moon." He turns the boar over, grunting in approval at the heaviness. "You did good, lad. We'll feast on wild pig this night and smoke the rest for later."

The crew gathers around the boar. I step back to examine the wound on my leg.

Ferdie watches me, smirking. "What did you do to yourself now, lad?"

Cook speaks up before I can answer. "Whilst you were sleeping the day away, the lad battled a great beast. You can thank him tonight when your belly is filled with wild pig."

"'Tis time he earned his keep," Gunther grumbles. "The Captain keeps him like a worthless pet."

"Your mouth spews words like a waterspout when the Captain and Peep are not nearby to hear," Cook says. "'Tis empty like a summer's well when they are."

The crew laughs uneasily. Gunther steps forward. "Do you challenge me on the boy's behalf?"

Cook stabs at the fire with a thick branch. "Remember who stews your food. A bit of this or that, and the pains in your stomach will drive you to madness."

Gunther spits into the flames and walks away without replying.

Jabbart waits until Gunther is out of earshot. "You are foolish to taunt him when the Captain is gone," he says. "There is no telling what he will do with no one to stop him."

Dabbing blood from my leg, I ask. "Where are the Captain and Peep?"

Jabbart shrugs. "Peep disappeared during the night. 'Tis strange that they are both gone at the same time."

Cook nods toward the boar. "We need to build a pit to smoke the meat before the sun rots it. Can you bring wood for a boucan by midday?"

Jabbart nods and turns to me. "Tend your injury and come help me, lad," he says. "When the Captain returns, he will order the ship careened. We must have the timber ready."

I wash my wound in the sea, wincing as I splash the salty water against my leg. I let the sun shine on it to dry the blood while I eat my biscuits. Then, I bandage it with a strip of cloth that Cook gives me. When Jabbart is ready, I follow him to the woods. At the charred oaks, I hesitate, reluctant to pass between them. No doubt the woods are full of wild pigs that will come at me again; I could not hope to fight another with an injured leg.

Jabbart squeezes my shoulder. "Overcome your fear," he says. "We'll be here too long for you to avoid the woods forever." He strides between the charred oaks without waiting for me to respond. Taking a deep breath, I fall in step behind him.

For the rest of the morning, we gather branches. Those too

thin or brittle are put aside for kindling. The thicker ones please Jabbart. Holding a fat oak branch in his hand, he explains how Cook will bind the branches with strong willows to build the boucan.

By midday we have what we need. Cook is waiting impatiently when we come out of the woods. He spreads the branches on the beach, crossing one over the other and binding them together at the corners with cut willows. When he finishes, he steps back and admires the three-sided structure he has built.

Flies have settled around the boar's eyes and snout, and Cook swats them away. He pulls a dagger from his pocket and hacks around the tusks. Then, with a quick twist of his wrists, he wrenches the ivory tusks free and tosses them to me. "With these in your pocket, the beast's strength will be with you always."

I wipe the bloodied tusks in the sand and stick them in my pocket. I don't believe they will bring me strength, but I have seen such tusks sold in the market in Charles Towne and know they hold value.

After skinning the boar, Cook gathers stones from the water's edge and arranges them inside the boucan. He stuffs dried grass between the stones and strikes a flint. The grass flames up. To my surprise, Cook and Jabbart quickly stomp out most of the fire, leaving just a few twigs burning between the stones. "If you roast the meat," Cook says, "you'll have to gobble it quick before it spoils. It's the smoke you want to cure the meat."

"Aye," Jabbart says. "Meat smoked proper will last for months. What we don't eat tonight will keep until it's gone."

Smoke slowly fills the boucan. Cook busies himself arranging the boar on the stones inside the boucan. I leave him to help Jabbart find wood to repair the ship and build a new mast.

Jabbart shows me how to look for proper trees. They cannot be too thick around the base or they will be unmanage-able. If the bark is brittle, the tree might be damaged and the wood might rot and split open at sea. There can be no mold, for that might spread to the other wood on the ship. Our search for just the right timber takes us deep into the woods. Along the way, Jabbart carves arrows on the trees to leave a trail for us to follow back. I watch, impressed. Such planning would never have occurred to me. Sometimes it seems as if there is too much to learn for me to ever become a sailor. Being a printer's son wasn't nearly as complicated.

Toward dusk, Jabbart finds an oak he thinks might do for the new mast. "Pine works best for the flooring and pins," he explains, "but oak stands strong against the wind."

Our search has taken us most of the day. With the canopy of branches above us, it is impossible to tell how much time has passed. As the sun sets and darkness falls, I begin to feel uneasy. I can barely see the ground in front of me. If a snake were lying across my path, I wouldn't know it until the creature had wrapped itself around my ankle.

"It grows late," I say to Jabbart. "We should mark the tree and come back for it tomorrow."

Jabbart agrees. "'Twill take a day or more to chop and carry out." He carves a wide X onto the tree's base so that it can easily be spotted the next day.

When we pass between the charred oaks, I see the glow from Cook's fire. Something strikes me as different, but in the darkness, I can't place what it is. Then, the fire roars to life and in the light of the flames I see that Peep and the Captain have returned.

CHAPTER FIFTEEN

The Captain greets us as we approach the fire. The night has grown cold and a damp wind blows in from the sea. With each gust the flames flicker, threatening to go out. "Beware of staying in the forest past dusk," he cautions as we join the circle. "It is unsafe once the stars appear." The remarks are made casually, as if he had not disappeared for a night and day.

Jabbart holds his hands above the flames to warm them. "Aye," he says. "'Twas by accident we stayed too long. We found nothing until we walked deep into the woods."

"Is what you found seaworthy?"

"A strong oak is marked for the mast," Jabbart replies, "but we'll need pine for the planking in the storage room."

"Start out early tomorrow," the Captain says. "The needles carpeting the forest floor tell me you will find the pine you need." Turning to me, he says, "You are to be congratulated on your victory this morning. Our stomachs will be full for many nights."

I smile at the compliment and accept a trencher from Cook. Thick slices of smoked meat float in gravy drippings scraped from the stones. Using my biscuit as a spoon, I scoop some up and place it in my mouth. The rich flavor spreads across my tongue, and I quickly take another bite.

Ferdie burps loudly and pats his stomach. "The beast whetted me appetite for fresh meat. With the boucan built, 'twould be a good time to fetch the animals off the ship."

Cook shakes his head. "Mayhap the chickens, but we need the goat for milk, and 'tis too soon to eat the pigs. Let them roam awhile and grow fat."

Solitaire Peep has remained silent until now. He glances quickly at the Captain before speaking to me. "The animals are in your care," he says sharply. "You should've fetched them from the ship already."

I stop eating, surprised at the rebuke. "I had no authority to do so," I say. "No one told me to fetch them."

"You should have thought of it yourself," Peep says, tapping his forehead. "I cain't be around always to tell you what to do."

The unfairness of Solitaire Peep's remarks cut me. It was not as if I had slept the day away. Had I not fought a wild pig and then helped to build a boucan to smoke it? Had I not walked in search of timber until my feet ached?

My tone hard, I say, "If you had told me to fetch the animals, I would have done so. Now that I know what you desire, I'll go for them at first light."

"You'll fetch them this night," Solitaire Peep snaps. "The moon will guide you."

Gunther laughs scornfully. "If you send the boy out alone on the longboat, 'tis likely he'll sink it. Mayhap I should row him over."

Gunther's suggestion alarms me. "No," I say quickly. "At dawn I can row over alone. The animals will keep until then."

"The animals must be fed daily or they will grow weak and sick," the Captain tells me. "Finish your meal and ready the longboat. I must tend to something onboard ship. We'll go tonight."

I push the last bite of meat into my mouth, grateful for something to fill it so that I can't answer back. I don't want to row out to the ship tonight. I'm sleepy and my leg hurts. If I did not have to tend the animals, I could ask Cook to make a poultice to soothe the wound. There will be no time to do that now. I return the trencher and start down the beach to where the boat is tied.

I glance back toward the camp as I pull the longboat toward the sea. The others have finished their meal and now rest on their pallets. Cook has tapped a small barrel of ale to fill their cups, and the crew's laughter carries across the wind.

I hold the boat steady so the Captain can board. The water is choppy, and the wind tosses the small vessel into the waves. Water sloshes over the boat's sides. I am glad the Captain has taken the lead position at the boat's bow, for I am not sure I could have handled the force of the wind. We row silently, not speaking until we are aboard the ship.

On deck, the Captain strikes a flint and lights two small tapers so that we can see. He hands one to me and I start for the storage room, but he stops me. "Come to my cabin first."

Inside, he pushes aside the papers on his desk and places the candle in a dish. It casts a dim glow inside the room. Motioning for me to sit, the Captain pulls out his log. He writes for several minutes before slamming the book shut. Stopping the ink bottle, he wipes his quill dry on a small cloth and sighs heavily. "Stop sulking, Jameson," he says. "It is behavior unbecoming a royal sailor."

"It is unfair how Solitaire Peep spoke to me," I say. "I have taken good care of the animals since you placed them in my care. Surely one day without food would not have harmed them." But as I speak the words I feel pangs of guilt, recalling how famished I had been on the streets of Charles Towne.

Stomach pangs led me to step into the bakery and pick up the loaf of bread. Hunger changed the path of my life, to be sure. "I shall not forget them again," I say.

The Captain nods. "Good, although your forgetfulness served my purpose well."

"I don't understand," I reply. "How is that?"

"I must speak to you of another matter, a private matter that could not be discussed on the island."

"Are you saying that you and Solitaire Peep played a ruse to get me here? That feeding the animals was an excuse?"

The Captain pushes back from his desk and walks over to the porthole. "You have surprised me over the last few months, Jameson," he says. "You've worked without complaint, and you've managed to stay one step ahead of Gunther, who would kill you given the chance."

I can't hide the surprise in my voice. "You knew that Gunther tormented me?"

"I knew," the Captain says. "But a man must find his own way. I told Peep that unless your life was in danger, we would not interfere."

"Is my life in danger now?" I ask. "Is that why you brought me here?"

"No," he replies, shaking his head. "I brought you here because I trust you to protect what belongs to Queen Anne." Unfastening a leather satchel, he pulls out a roll of papers bound by thin strips of leather. "These are the maps of a new world, Jameson," he says. "When I return to England and show them to Her Majesty, she will send royal protectors to claim the land in her name and armies to defend it."

My eyes widen as the maps are spread wide upon the desk. I have never seen such drawings. Each map shows detailed markings that could easily guide a ship's captain.

"You gaze upon my life's work," the Captain says. "These

maps will ensure that England rules this new world. England and England alone."

I touch the maps gently. Though my eyes are not as trained as my father's had been, I can see that each map is a work of art, one that could never be replaced.

"Whose work is this?" I ask, my voice filled with awe.

"Mine and other artists who have sailed with me," he replies. "But that's not important right now."

"What is it that you want me to do?" I ask, raising my eyes to meet his.

The Captain rolls up the maps and reties them. He doesn't speak for so long that I think that he has changed his mind. "You are a curious lad," he says suddenly. "Surely you've wondered where Solitaire Peep and I disappeared to."

I shrug. "Solitaire Peep claims my nose is too long. I did not want to ask."

The Captain laughs. "It was Peep's own long nose that led us to the place on the island where he will soon take you. A place hidden deep in the woods."

"Sir?"

The Captain stands. "Be ready, Jameson. That is all I will say at this time. When the hour is right, Solitaire Peep will take you there. You must follow without comments that will alert the others."

My head swirls and questions are ready to spill from my mouth, but the Captain waves me silent. "I'll say no more than this. The maps before you will be used to secure England's place in the New World. Until I can return, they must be hidden in a place that will keep them safe from harm.

"And you think harm will come to them soon?" I ask quietly.

"We are within our enemy's reach and soon the weather will turn against us. Had the Spanish merchant not attacked,

we would not be in this predicament. Now *Destiny* is in peril."
He pauses. "Am I right to trust you with England's future,
Jameson? You, above all the others who sail on my ship?"

I stare at the maps spread out before me, still awed by the
perfect lettering and drawing. Even without knowing their
value to Queen Anne, I would have protected them from harm.

I nod firmly. "I can be trusted," I reply.

"I pray you speak the truth, Jameson. Because if I've mis-
judged you, God help us both. Betray me and our heads will
adorn a pike on London Bridge."

I swallow hard. My mouth feels dry as I speak. "I will follow Peep without question," I say, "and I shall tell no one
where I go or what I see. I give you my word."

CHAPTER SIXTEEN

Two mornings after the animals are brought to shore, we guide *Destiny* into shallow waters and carefully tip her onto her side so that we can scrape her clean from bow to stern. Peep orders me to start beneath the bow, but I have flicked off only a few barnacles with my dagger when he suddenly changes his mind and says I must help Cook and Ratty Tom catch and salt fish to carry with us when we sail to Charles Towne. I start to protest that I am capable of doing more than salting fish but then I see Gunther checking the ropes that hold our ship in place. Peep changed my orders, I think, for the purpose of protecting me. My head could have easily ended up squashed like a melon if Gunther had found a way to let the ship fall on top of me.

The food supplies have dwindled so low that the crew now grumbles when they see what fills their bowls each night, and Cook is intent on filling every empty barrel with fish.

Ratty Tom and I head down the beach away from the noise of the crew at work on the ship, walking until all we can hear are waves crashing onto the shore. Then, we wade out into the sea up to our chins to sink our nets. After they are in place, we move closer to the shore and begin to fish, using poles that Jabbart made out of strong saplings he found in the forest, with bent nails for hooks.

This becomes a daily routine. Each morning we search out a new place along the shoreline to sink our nets and cast out our fishing lines. The fish seem to have a taste for the fat brown wrigglers that we dig after each afternoon rain and the tiny crabs that run along the shore each night just before the moon appears. I have concocted a treat for them of two worms wrapped around a crab, with the hook through the middle.

We fish from dawn to dusk, taking time only to eat the meager rations Cook sends with us for our noon meal. My arm aches from casting out my line, and the skin on my chest peels off in wide pieces from where I have sizzled beneath the sun. Cook visits us throughout the day to gather the fish we have placed on strings for him. He takes the fish back to our camp to smoke some in the boucan and salt the rest. Fish has become our breakfast, lunch, and supper, with little else alongside it. A few days ago, though, Cook trapped three wild birds and a fat squirrel, which he stewed with wild onions. To go along with that, he scraped out the fat that lined the squirrel's carcass and used it to flavor several bunches of jagged green leaves topped with yellow flowers that he found just inside the woods. The change was welcomed, and though we wished for more, no one complained.

Yesterday, when we pulled in our nets at sunset, a loggerhead turtle larger than any I have ever seen peered back at me with wet black eyes. Cook whooped when he saw it. Though I felt bad to know its fate, I cannot deny that the meat, sweet with just a hint of the salty sea, made me long to catch another one the next day. Cook cut the meat from the shell and then chopped it into thick chunks, which he divided evenly amongst the crew. For supper, we speared the turtle meat with our daggers and roasted it over the fire, along with long slivers of the rattlesnake that Jabbart killed while searching for more kindling.

We have been on Crossed Island almost two moons, and Jabbart finished the new mast last night. After breakfast, Peep calls the crew together to help pull the mast down the beach to where *Destiny*, scraped clean, waits.

There is much grunting and shouting as we hoist the mast into place. A high tide helps us to get the ship upright and into the water. With Peep's permission, Cook untaps a new barrel of ale and our cups are filled in celebration. We raise our cups to the sky as the Captain offers a toast to his ship, that she always stay ahead of our enemies and that she remains sea-worthy as we sail from this place. We stand on the beach with the sea swirling around our ankles and drink the warm ale, our eyes upon *Destiny* as she floats offshore with her new mast. Jabbart boasts that England's finest shipbuilder could not have done a better job nor used a stronger wood. I sense he feels a pride much like I did whenever I penned perfect letters for my father. They are alike in some ways, I think, the molding of wood and words.

With *Destiny* back in the water and ready to sail, I sense we will soon leave Crossed Island. Lightning flashes against the sky daily now, and last night I slept poorly because of the loud rumbling of thunder. Cook says a fierce storm nears. The signs are everywhere. The trees along the wood's edge bend and sway in the wind, as if preparing for an assault. And I've never seen quite so many lizards—long green ones the color of the stones in Peep's patch and tiny yellow ones with black stripes. They scurry back and forth across the sand, as if uncertain as to which way to go. The pigs and goat have roamed free in the woods since being brought from the ship, and we have not seen them in days, not since the winds started blowing hard. Jabbart and Ferdie have tried to catch them, but the animals are too cunning for them and will not let themselves be trapped. Perhaps the pigs sense that the boucan awaits them, but Peep says the goat will sail with us to Charles Towne, for Cook craves her milk to make his stews and broths.

For the first time, our nets came up empty today. Cook claims it's because the fish sense the storm and seek safety by swimming deeper into the ocean. He says, "When nature's frightened, man should take heed." There is worry in his voice. At supper, I overhear him whisper to Peep that we should set sail soon, before a storm destroys our ship and maroons us here with no food.

The winds make it hard to keep the fire lit, and the rain that began at dusk has become so forceful that we must shout to one another to be heard. There was talk of sleeping on the ship to shield us from the weather, but Solitaire Peep said we will be stuck on the ship soon enough. There are no games of dice in the sand tonight, and I turn in early with others, bedding beneath four sails that have been tied together and secured to the ground with thick stakes. Peep assigns me a spot near the outer edge where the wind blows rain on me, but I do not complain; in truth, there is no guarantee of shelter for any of us. Before morning the wind will likely sweep the sails out to sea.

The sound of the rain beating upon the sails and the waves crashing into the shoreline drowns out all else during the night. Though I wish I could sketch the dancing of the tall grass upon the dunes and the waves, tall and tipped silver in the moonlight, the gusts would rip the parchment from my hands. Instead, I turn my back to the wind, pull my knees closer to my chest, and close my eyes.

I bolt upright as a hand clamps down hard across my mouth. I grab at the hand and struggle, until Peep holds his lantern to his face. He places his finger before his lips and jerks his head toward the woods. When I nod, he moves silently into the darkness.

My heart pounds as I pull on my boots. So many nights have passed since my conversation with the Captain that I thought he had changed his mind. Beneath the sails, the others snore loudly. The heavy rain muffles the sound of my movements as I pull on my boots. I duck from beneath the sail, and follow the light from Peep's lantern down the beach. The wind is fierce, and it shoves me along as if I am its prisoner. My hair blows about wildly, stinging my face; I push the locks aside and grope for the rawhide I use to gather them together, but it is gone, lost somewhere along the beach.

Thick clouds hide the moon, but the flickering light from the lantern guides me down the long stretch of sand to the woods. When Solitaire Peep rounds the bend in the beach, the light dims and I quicken my steps.

The beach grows dark suddenly, and I know Peep has stepped between the charred oaks, where the dense foliage hides the lantern's light. I enter the woods a few moments later and see him standing beneath the wide branch of an oak tree. "Hurry, boy," Peep snaps, stepping forward. "'Twill be dawn in a few hours and there's work to be done."

Peep carries a leather satchel that I recognize as the one from the Captain's cabin. Tossing me a small shovel, Peep says, "Follow me and keep up. If you become lost, you'll stay that way."

Despite the darkness and the thick tangle of trees and shrubs, we walk at a quick pace. My legs tire, but I don't dare slow down. The rain is so heavy the canopy of trees can't shield us. The ground turns soggy beneath my feet and twice I stumble, but Solitaire Peep continues on, never once looking back to see if I'm keeping up. Curiosity and fear of being left behind push me forward. I have never been so deep into the woods.

As dawn nears, the walking becomes easier. The space between the trees and shrubs widens. Suddenly the woods open up, and we are on the beach. I look around in surprise. "We have walked in circles!" I shout, cupping my hand to my mouth so that he can hear me above the roar of the wind and the crashing of waves onto the shore.

"Nay, lad," Peep says. "We have crossed through the woods to the other side of the island. There's nothing beyond but sea."

Wiping the rain from my eyes, I see a rocky overhang stretching from the woods into the water. It is the cliff I saw from the ship when we first came, I think, surprised that I had forgotten it until that moment.

Solitaire Peep hands me the leather satchel and wades into the water, his thin body leaning forward against the wind. The water is just below his waist when he reaches the cliff. He grabs a handful of the vines that hang from the rock. With a dozen or so quick swipes, he thins them out. He wipes away the rain streaming down his face and beckons me into the surf. "Bring me the satchel, boy, and keep your hands wrapped tight around it!"

I hold the satchel above my head and wade out to Peep. He snatches it from me and holds it safely above the water. With the other hand, he grabs the vines he has left hanging and pulls them to the side.

My eyes grow wide when I see the narrow opening gouged into the cliff's side. "A secret cave," I whisper.

"Aye, 'tis that," Solitaire Peep says smugly. "And only two people know it exists: me and the Captain. Not even Queen Anne..." He stops and his good eye begins to twitch. He turns so quickly that he almost knocks me over. Grabbing my collar, he yanks me close. "Breathe a word of this to another living soul, and you'll rue the day you were born," Peep says. "The Captain will cut out your wagging tongue and use it for a hair ribbon. Get my meaning, boy?"

I push him away. His breath smells of the clams Cook served for the evening meal. "Get your hands off me," I say. "I gave the Captain my word that I wouldn't tell what happens on this night."

Peep lets his hands fall to his side. "Let's step quick then," he says. "The others will grow suspicious if they wake before we return." Grabbing the satchel, he turns sideways and squeezes through the gap. A shiver runs down my back as I follow him into the cave.

CHAPTER SEVENTEEN

The light from Solitaire Peep's lantern flickers suddenly. He stops and shields it with his hand. "Stay still for a minute, boy," he whispers, looking around as if he is trying to decide which way to go.

My eyes adjust gradually to the darkness. It is humid inside the cave and the moldy smell makes it difficult to breathe. I sneeze twice, startled when the sound echoes back to me. A sudden flapping of wings overhead makes me gasp and duck. I press my hand against the wall to steady myself, and I feel slime beneath my palm. Wiping my hand against my breeches, I follow Peep's lead and step around a small pool of water. Whatever we are here for must be done quickly, so we can leave this foul place.

Peep moves cautiously, his hand cupped around the mouth of the lantern. I know he is being careful not to risk our only source of light. I follow silently behind, the shovel gripped tightly in my hands. Every few steps, Solitaire Peep stops and listens; I listen too, but all I hear is water dripping down the cave's walls and the flight of winged creatures I cannot see.

The ground twists and turns with some passages so narrow that we must press against the wall to pass through. After walking for a while, we approach an incline where the floor seems to tilt upward. The passage widens, and we come to a large space; two stone ledges protrude from the side of each wall, as if the middle above our heads had been cut away. Solitaire Peep stops and looks around. His patch gleams in the darkness. "We'll work here," he says. Reaching up, he drops the satchel onto the widest of the two ledges, Turning to me, he jerks his thumb toward the ledge. "Hoist yourself up and be quick!"

Tossing the spade onto the ledge, I clutch the ledge with both hands and pull myself up halfway until the slab presses against my stomach. Peep grabs my ankles and boosts me over the edge. He hands the lantern up to me, and I place it against the wall where it won't get knocked over. Then I stand and brush the dirt from my hands onto my breeches. Peep pulls himself up beside me. His nostrils twitch as the smell of clay and mold fills them. "Take a sniff, boy," he says. "Smells like the earth itself. 'Tis the perfect spot." He looks around, studying the area, as if he has lost something, and then points to the base of the back wall. "Get to work. Dig a deep spot there."

I open my mouth to ask why, and then think better of it. If I ask, Solitaire Peep will simply tell me my nose is too long. Besides, the sooner we finish what we have to do, the sooner we can return. Dropping to my knees, I jam the spade into the crevice between the floor and wall. The dirt is hard as stone, and it takes all my strength to chip away the smallest amount.

Soon, I've dug out a small crevice. Peep holds the satchel against it. When he sees that the hole is still too small, he begins to rant. "Dig faster, you lazy good-for-nothing!" His tone is harsh, and when I stop to rest, he gives me a hard kick in the legs to spur me on.

I lift my head and snap, "I can work faster if you do not cripple me."

I try to hurry, but the wind surges through the cave. Every now and then, I hear a noise that makes me stop digging and wonder about the source. Could a tree have snapped from the force of the wind? Or has lightning struck one of the tall oaks in the woods? There is no way to see out, but I can tell the storm is a bad one.

I look up and shiver. Dampness has eased into my bones and they ache. The lantern's light throws shadows upon the sweating walls. I dig harder, anxious to leave.

Finally, I wipe my hands on my muddy breeches and stand. "There, I've done a good job of it."

Solitaire Peep snorts. "Don't be getting ahead of yourself. Time will tell what kind of job you did." He kneels and sticks his hand inside the hole. Satisfied it is deep enough, he grabs the leather satchel, holding it up for me to see. "'Tis England's future inside this leather, lad," he says. "Maps of a New World. Pray God these walls keep them safe."

I draw a deep breath, remembering the Captain's words. For weeks I have sketched what I thought to be maps intended to lead England's ships to new ports. Instead, I have drawn territories that could be seized in Queen Anne's name to give England a stronghold in the New World. If the satchel falls into enemy hands, France or Spain will rule the New World.

Solitaire Peep shoves me aside. He covers the satchel with loose dirt and fills the hole. Using the water running down the side of the wall, he smoothes the edges until there is no sign the wall has been altered. He brushes his hand over the wet clay. "Should dry within the hour, boy," he whispers. "The old blending with the new. And only you, me, and the Captain will ever be the wiser."

I squat beside Solitaire Peep and run my fingertips along the wall. Wasn't it just like Peep to take all the credit? He's right, though. No one will ever know. "Aye," I say. "We can sail for one year or for ten. Time matters not, for it will await our return."

Solitaire Peep doesn't answer. His face grows tight and his eye begins to twitch. "Did you hear that?" he asks.

I listen for a moment but hear nothing unusual. "It's only the wind blowing," I say.

Peep waits a few moments and then nods. "You could be right. Just me nerves, that's all."

"Best we start back," I say. I jump down from the ledge. Peep passes the lantern carefully down to me.

"Hold up, boy," Peep says, dropping down beside me. "We won't get far with the storm outside. What say we rest here for a while before starting back?"

"Won't the Captain expect us back soon?" I ask, anxious to leave the cave.

"If we leave now, the sea will try to snatch you up," he says. I don't want to be toting you on my back because the waves are covering your head." He drops the shovel at his feet. "We'll wait a bit until the winds ease."

As if the matter is settled, he sits down on the floor and leans his head back against the wall.

Sighing, I place the lantern on the ledge and sit beside him. Arguing with Peep is pointless.

Though the wind shrieks loudly outside the cave, Peep dozes off quickly. Closing my eyes, I try to drown out the sounds of the storm so that I can rest too. My arms hurt from burying the satchel, and yesterday I worked hard rigging sails to the new mast.

I drift off into an uneasy sleep. I dream I am standing by the ship's railing scooping up buckets of water. I cannot work fast enough. Black water pours over the ship's sides and swirls around my legs. It rises to my knees and then to my waist. I bail faster: up and over, up and over, but still the water grows deeper, until it reaches my neck. I open my mouth to scream and the sea pours in.

I awake choking. Water covers the floor. I give Peep a hard shake. "Get up!"

He jerks awake and looks around. He pats the floor around him, and then licks his palm. "'Tis salt," he says, his eye growing wide. "'Tis the sea, boy. The sea has come to us!"

I shake my head, trying to remain calm. "It's just a little flooding because of the storm," I say. "Come on. We'll go back the way we came. Look, the water's only at our knees. If we hurry, there's time."

I grab the lantern from the ledge and turn back toward the cave's entrance. The water is heavy against my legs, but I keep moving. When it has risen to my waist, I raise the lantern above my head. Peep splashes along beside me, his bony legs struggling against the rushing water.

Soon, the water is almost at my chest. I try to move forward, but the force of it pushes me back. "Move closer to the wall and edge ahead!" I yell to Peep. "Don't try to walk in the middle!"

"Hold the lantern my way, boy!" he croaks. "I cain't see!"

I grip the lantern tighter as we move through a narrow section. Behind me, Peep walks close behind, tugging on my shirt so that he is close to the light. The cave twists and turns, and after several minutes, I stop to get my bearings. I hold the light high in front of me to try and gauge the direction we must go. In the flickering light, I see that the cave splits not too far ahead. I turn my head to tell Peep that we are almost at the entrance, when a roaring fills the cave. Peep pushes me, urging me to keep moving, but I hesitate, unsure of this noise that is suddenly all around me. As I move forward, a wall of water rushes from one side of the cave. I shout a warning to Peep and press against the wall to try and get out of its path, but it's too late. The water crashes into me, tearing the lantern from my hand. I lunge for it, but the rushing water carries it away.. Horrified, I watch as the lantern disappears. Peep's fingers claw at my arm. I reach out and grab him, trying to hold on to him, but the current is too strong and too fast, and he is ripped away. Within seconds, he is gone. I can see nothing now except a swirling mass of black seawater as it roars past me.

"Peep!" I scream.

But he doesn't answer. A deep darkness fills the cave. I cling to the wall, calling out for him again and again, but the sound of water churning past me and the echo of my own words are all that I hear.

I turn back to go after him, bracing myself against the wall so that I can stay on my feet. I move deeper into the cave, screaming out Peep's name. Perhaps he is just around a turn, waiting to yell at me for losing the lantern. I can go only a few feet before I am forced to turn back. The water is almost at my shoulders. I push on in the darkness, one hand against the wall, and the other an oar that I use to push the water from me. With every step, I call out, hoping Peep is behind me, but all I hear is the sound of rushing water.

After a while, the water rushing past me slows, and the sounds inside the cave begin to change. I am still yelling for Peep when I hear someone call my name. I think I am imagining it, for the voice comes from in front of me. I stop moving and press against the cave wall, peering into the darkness. Then, a gash of light falls over me, and I see the vine-covered gouge in the wall Peep and I climbed through. Forcing himself through the narrow gap is the Captain.

CHAPTER EIGHTEEN

Two days after the storm, we pull anchor and sail from Crossed Island beneath calm winds. I stay up on deck until we round the bend and the cliff comes into view. Looking quickly away, I whisper a prayer that Peep will rest in peace.

The first day at sea is hectic as the crew adjusts to life back onboard. I keep busy and turn my mind from what happened in the cave. But when night falls, the thoughts jumble together inside my head and I cannot sleep. I close my eyes, and once again I am pressed against the cave's wall, feeling Peep's hands on my arm. The Captain says I am not responsible for his death, but his words sound hollow, for I am here and Peep is not. Sometimes, I forget that he is gone. In the morning I awake and hear a voice overhead. For a moment, I think it is Peep calling out orders. Then I remember.

News of Peep's death shocked the crew. The Captain did not tell them the truth, only that Peep had taken me to the other side of the island to seek the goat and piglets so that we might bring them onboard ship. There, he said, Peep was swept into the surf by a raging tide. It was a weak lie that no one believed. Gunther's scowl said as much, though he wouldn't dare question the Captain. When we were alone, Cook asked me if Peep had suffered. I said nothing, for I did not want to remember.

Crossed Island suffered greatly from the storm's wrath. Trees were felled on both sides of the island, and dunes flattened into the sand. Had the Captain not come to the cave in search of us, it is unlikely I would have been able to trace my steps back to the other side, for the path Peep and I took no longer existed.

The ship seems quieter now, and the storage room no longer feels the same without the animals. I like to think they are safe on Crossed Island. At night, when sleep won't come, I imagine the goat, my first friend onboard ship, nibbling the tall grass that grows between the charred oaks, and the pigs rolling about as they sun themselves on the white sandy beach.

On our fourth night at sea, the Captain and Cook come down to inventory the food stores. Earlier at supper, the grumblings of the crew grew loud when Cook ladled the watery soup into their trenchers. We have no more than a week's worth of flour left, and so little meat that Cook stews it now for broth, as there is not enough to serve for meals. The fish we salted is gone and Cook's net contains nothing these days save for seaweed and shells and, if we are lucky, a few crab claws. He claims the fish that sought refuge from the storm deep in the ocean are taking their time coming to the surface again. The Captain says the storage room will be filled soon, for a letter of credit bearing Queen Anne's signature is registered in Charles Towne. He will purchase supplies as soon as we dock.

A surprise greets me when I go up on deck on our sixth day at sea, for we have arrived at the mouth of Charles Towne's harbor. Though for months I have dreamed of returning home, I feel sick in my stomach when I see the steeple atop the meeting house.

At the Captain's orders, Jabbart hoists the Queen's standards. We are noticed immediately. Within the hour, two merchants send messages by longboat offering their goods for sale and asking what goods we have brought. I hide near the bow and stay out of sight. Last night, I thought to protest when the Captain said I must stay below deck once the ship drops anchor. Who would see me now and think of the boy who ran away? My hair falls past my shoulders, and I stand tall even in bare feet. But the memory of Charles Towne's jail lingers still, and so I do as I am told and conceal myself without complaint.

Across the deck, Ferdie tosses aside the sail he has spent two days mending and strides toward me. He shoves me hard on the arm. "So, you're back home," he says. "Are you standing here planning how to sneak off the ship?"

I shrug. I have no plans to sneak anywhere, but it is my business to know that, not his.

Spitting into the water, Ferdie says, "Best not let Gunther see you wasting time. I heard him tell you to mend the fish nets."

"Reknotting the nets is your duty" I reply, glancing over at the till, where Gunther stands. With Peep gone, Gunther has taken over the job of steering the ship and passing out assignments each morning. So far, the Captain hasn't interfered, though I wish he would. I am sick of Gunther's commands. I raise my voice. "You should do your own work and stop pushing it off on others."

Grinning, Ferdie yells over to Gunther, "The lad says you can mend the nets yourself since you do little else."

Gunther doesn't look at me. Another ship has entered his view and his eyes are upon it. Over his shoulder, he says, "You've wasted the morning, boy. Knot the nets before supper or you'll go hungry."

Lifting my chin, I say, "I'll eat as I do every night. What right have you to lord it over me or anyone else?"

Scowling, he swats at a fly that buzzes near his head. "Old One-Eye is dead, thanks to the devil's luck you brought upon this ship. From hereon, I'll carry out his duties. Best watch your tongue if you desire to keep it in your head."

I swallow hard, but when I speak my voice is calm. "It is not my fault Solitaire Peep drowned, but I have no need to explain that to you. You have no right to assume his position as second-in-command."

I can feel the eyes of the crew on me. A few oarsmen mumble in agreement, but a fierce glance from Gunther silences them. I can see that they believe Gunther to be in charge. I clear my throat and say loudly, "If you truly were second-in-command, you would know that the nets are mended by Ferdie. Peep would not have forgotten such a simple thing."

Gunther hands the tiller off to Jabbart. I know he is coming for me, but I stand my ground. With three long strides he is upon me. He grabs me by my hair and yanks me so close that his mouth brushes my ear. "I've stood silent whilst you brought bad luck to this ship. Had the Captain heeded my warning, we would not have lost the mast in battle and Peep would not have drowned. Do not close your eyes tonight, brat, or it will be the last time that you do."

Over Gunther's shoulder, I see the hatch lift and glimpse a scarlet plume. Ferdie sees it, too. He moves quickly away as the Captain comes onto the deck, dressed in full uniform for our arrival in Charles Towne.

Gunther has not released the hold he has on my hair. Grimacing in pain, I say, "I've my own work to do. You'll have to find someone else to reknot the nets."

Gunther reaches for the dagger at his side. Without loosening his grip on me, he pulls the knife free and holds it up before him. "You've pushed me too far," he says. "There's no reason to wait for night to fall. Refusing to obey a royal officer is a dying offense."

"Who is it that he has refused to obey?" the Captain asks loudly. "I've given him no command."

Gunther's hands fall from me. He turns around slowly. "I told the boy to see to the nets so they are ready when we need them again."

"Mending the nets is Ferdie's job," the Captain says. "Why is it that you've asked Jameson to do another's work?"

Gunther clears his throat and spits over the railing. Not bothering to wipe the spit from his mouth, he says, "We are short on crew. The boy needs to do as he is told without question."

"Jameson does as I command," the Captain responds. "And I do not recall assigning him any new duties this morning."

Gunther scowls. "This boy who stumbles at every turn is not fit to serve our Queen. Moreover, 'tis bad luck to bring a brat onboard ship. You should have known better. Anyone would have to be daft to believe him sixteen as he claims."

The crew gasps at the insult, but the Captain holds his temper. "His age no longer matters. The boy has proven himself worthy to sail on a royal vessel and to serve our Queen."

"Peep is dead and our mast destroyed in a battle caused by the lad's bumbling. He flaunted himself to the enemy and spoiled our ruse. You should have tossed him overboard then."

"I could say our mast was destroyed because of your lack of skill, Gunther. Had your aim been true, the enemy ship would not have been able to return fire. If there is blame to be placed, perhaps it should be placed with you."

A few men laugh loudly, pleased to see Gunther put in his place.

Gunther's face darkens. He fingers the dagger still in his hand. Before he can speak, the Captain says, "Put the knife away and get back to your duties. I give the commands and no one else."

Gunther smiles. "You will need a first mate with Peep gone. 'Tis natural that it be me. I have served you longest."

The Captain shakes his head. "Your actions these past few

days do not please me. You command as if you think yourself a king." The Captain's voice has turned cold. "You are not."

Aware he has gone too far, Gunther bows slightly. "I assume no such thing. If I have displeased you, then I must redeem myself. Tell me what it is you would have me do."

"You are to leave this ship immediately when we drop anchor and seek out merchants who can fill our hold quickly. I have no desire to linger in port."

"I'll prepare to take my leave, then. Perhaps the boy can take the ship in to the wharf." He grins at me. "Surely those who watch us approach will be glad to see the return of their long-lost son."

The Captain sighs. "I grow weary of your attempts at wit, Gunther. When you return, I may consider putting you in irons for a night or two to cool your tongue. Go now and ask Cook for a list of what we need."

Gunther glances around quickly, as if taking note of those who have witnessed his defeat. Most of the crew lower their heads, but my eyes meet his and I hold his gaze until he moves toward the hatch. When he has below, I take a deep breath. I feel a growing sense of dread. "He will kill me," I say, "given the chance."

The Captain nods. "Aye, that he will. When he leaves the ship, come to my cabin. In the meantime, lock the storage door when you go below and do not be caught alone."

Placing his arm around my shoulder, he nods toward Charles Towne. "This is your home, Jameson, but I fear you sail toward great risk, both on ship and off. You must watch your step, so that someday you can celebrate your sixteenth birthday."

My head jerks up. "How long have you known?"

The Captain takes off his hat and pulls the feather through his hands. "I've had my suspicions since that first day when you fell at my feet."

"I did not set out to lie to you," I say quickly. "But I was afraid for my life."

"I do not abide lying, Jameson. A man who cannot be trusted is worthless to me. But you are right. Had you confessed you were not sixteen, I would not have allowed you to sail on the *Destiny*."

"Would you have allowed the crew to toss me overboard?" I ask.

The Captain raises an eyebrow. "That is something we both must wonder about. I did not know you then as I do now." He pauses and then adds, "Your life may well depend on your wits, Jameson. Mind what I say and stay out of sight. We will dock for two days to fill our hold and then set sail. Sixteen or not, I desire that you sail with me when we go."

"I shall be extra cautious, sir. When *Destiny* sails from Charles Towne, I will be onboard."

CHAPTER NINETEEN

I can hardly believe I am home. We dropped anchor late yesterday, and I went below, for fear that a merchant using his spyglass would catch a glimpse of me. Last night, Gunther rowed to shore to organize supplies to be brought to ship. The Captain says we will leave the night before market day, before the port is clogged by ships arriving to trade.

Near supper, Cook bade me to bring the Captain a tankard of ale. I found him alone in his cabin, plotting the route we will take when we leave Charles Towne. I felt a shock to my core when I saw myself in the shaving mirror hanging on the wall behind his desk. My hair is bleached white as bones left to dry in the sun and my skin is deeply browned. My cheekbones jut forth, the skin stretched taut over them like cloth upon a loom.

The ship is quiet this night. I have passed much of it looking through the porthole, which draws me to it like a needle is pulled north on a compass. The stars cast their crystals upon the Ashley River and the water sparkles beneath me as I press my face against the glass and watch Charles Towne sleep. A few candles still burn, and I wonder if one glows from the window of the print shop.

Were I able to step foot on land, I would walk past the street where the print shop sits and on to the city field, where the bodies of those taken by the plague were buried. I know not where in the field my father and mother lie, for the dead numbered many and most were not placed in marked ground. It would be enough, I think, to stand still and whisper to them that I have come home, at least for a brief spell, and that I am alive and well. I would tell them that I have spent my time recording for Queen Anne, and that someday I will fill sheets of parchment with the stories of the days I sailed with the infamous Attack Jack and his one-eyed mate, Solitaire Peep. My father would know then that though I now labor at sea, I have not forgotten our trade. In my heart, I am still a printer's son.

🎗🎗

Three mornings later, a fierce pounding causes me to jump from my pallet and grab for my breeches and shirt. For a moment, I think the noise is cannon fire and I am being summoned to battle. When the pounding resumes, I remember that I am in the storage room. This is the last day we will be in Charles Towne. By nightfall, the hold will be filled and we will sail on the next morning's tide.

Jabbart bursts through the door, fastening the buttons on his blue coat as he enters. He is dressed in full uniform, a sight I have never before seen. Jabbart speaks rapidly. "I came to warn you not to stray above deck before dark," he says. "The Captain is leaving the ship and there will be no one to speak for you if you are spotted."

I button my shirt quickly, surprised at the news. "Why does he leave?" I ask.

"To search for Gunther. No merchants have come onboard to say they have spoken to him; the Captain fears he may have met with harm."

"I heard the crew talking last night," I say. "There is much guessing about Gunther's absence."

"We will search the streets, and if need be, go to the constable's house."

"Perhaps Gunther drank too much ale and has fallen asleep in a tavern," I say.

Jabbart shakes his head. "The Captain thinks he may have been taken aboard another ship. His gunnery skills are widely known." At the door, he turns back with a final warning. "Stay out of sight, Jameson. Word will spread that Gunther is missing, and attention will fall on *Destiny*."

After Jabbart leaves, I shake the dust from my pallet and flip it onto the clean side. Without Gunther around to plague me, the time has passed easily. I do not have to look over my shoulder when I walk through the dark hallway to use the night bucket, nor do I spring up from my sleep every time a mouse scurries along the floorboard. I cannot be the only one who is glad Gunther is gone, for the mood on board has been light. That the Captain would delay *Destiny*'s departure to search for him speaks of Gunther's value to Queen Anne's cause; the Captain places his duty to her above all else.

For the remainder of the day, I keep busy below deck, repairing the hammocks that show signs of wear. I pull out rotted thread and weave in fresh hemp rope. The job requires concentration. If I allow my mind to wander, a tangled mess quickly reminds me to attend to the task at hand.

The work makes the day pass quickly. The ringing of the supper bell catches me by surprise. On the second ring, I stand and stretch. My back aches from bending over the roping. Still, if there were another hammock to be retied, I would do it just to avoid going to my room.

The storage room is too quiet without the animals. I have no wish to spend another night with only my growling stomach to keep me company. The food stores have dwindled to nothing. Since arriving in port, we have eaten only what Cook catches each morning. Yesterday, Cook scraped oysters from the rock piles along the beach. The bucket he filled barely fed the crew. I long for the hold to be refilled and food to be plentiful again.

I reluctantly put away the mended hammocks and take my supper below deck. I sit on my pallet and eat the meager ration of boiled fish and beans Cook left for me. Gradually the light fades until I am in darkness. Only then do I go up on deck, breathing deeply of the fresh air until the cold air stings my throat.

The crew mills about, but I do not join them. Instead, I lean over the railing and let the wet breeze sweep across my face. The air smells of salt and muck. Lanterns glow from across the water. Tonight the citizens will stay up late preparing their goods to trade or sell at market tomorrow.

Jabbart and the Captain have not returned, but I am not worried. They have likely found Gunther and have lingered to eat a bountiful dinner. I imagine them seated at a table before a crackling tavern fire, as a servant girl fills their trenchers with juicy strips of peppered meat and bread that drips with melted butter. My stomach growls noisily, and I try to think of something other than food. The pangs in my gut remind me of the days following my parent's deaths, when I wandered Charles Towne's streets alone and hungry.

As the night passes, the lights across the bay dim; one by one, the crew drifts below deck. A heavy rain begins to fall, and I pull my collar higher, unwilling to go to my room. I am still at the railing when the sound of oars slapping water drives me back into the shadows. From my hiding place, I watch the longboat approach. The man at the helm has his head bent against the rain. When he lifts it, I recognize Jabbart. I fetch the grappling hook and run back to the railing to pull him alongside.

I gasp when Jabbart steps onboard. His sleeve is ripped

from the shoulder. His left eye is swollen shut and dried blood stains his cheek.

"What happened?" I ask.

"The Captain has been arrested," Jabbart says, rubbing his hands together nervously. "I managed to fight my way free, but he was surrounded and I could not get to him." In a weary voice, he explains what happened when he and the Captain arrived in Charles Towne. "We searched for Gunther all morning. Finally, we went to the constable to seek assistance. Instead of helping us, he called the guards."

"And?" I say, growing impatient to hear the rest of the story. "Where is Gunther now?"

"We never found Gunther," Jabbart says. "'Tis the Captain they seized…for piracy."

I frown. "You are not making sense. Did you hit your head?"

"The captain of the Spanish merchant who destroyed our mast sailed to Charles Towne for repairs," Jabbart says. "He filed a complaint with the constable, claiming *Destiny* is a pirating vessel."

Relieved, I smile. "That's easy to disprove. Spain is the enemy of our Queen. The Captain fired against the Spanish merchant in her name."

"No," Jabbart says. "When we battled the Spanish merchant, we were no longer at war. Whist we were at sea, Queen Anne signed a treaty at Utrecht. Our Captain broke Queen Anne's promise of peace to France and Spain."

"A treaty with Spain and France?" I say, amazed at the idea. The idea of England allying itself with France and Spain seems unbelievable.

Jabbart sways slightly, and I quickly reach out to steady him. "Come below. We can talk whilst Cook tends your eye. Then you should rest."

"I'm hungry and tired to the bone, but there's no time for sleep. We must think of a way to save the Captain."

"We can do nothing this night," I say, looking across the bay. "Charles Towne sleeps. You must sleep, too."

Jabbart grabs my arm so hard I wince. "You don't understand, lad," he says. "Our Captain has been accused of piracy. On Wednesday, he goes before the court to answer the charge."

"Yes, and they will hear his story and set him free."

"No," Jabbart says. "His friends in Charles Towne are few. They know him only as Attack Jack, who for years has taken what he has needed in the name of Queen Anne. Are you not proof of that?"

I think back to my first day on ship when I had pleaded to be returned to Charles Towne. Waving the Letter of Marque, the Captain had refused.

"The Letter of Marque!" I say quickly. "It was signed by Queen Anne herself."

Jabbart's eyes widen. "Where have you seen such a letter?"

"In the Captain's desk," I say, heading toward the hatch. "At first light, we shall bring the constable royal proof that the Captain had Queen Anne's permission to attack the Spanish ship."

When I reach the Captain's door, I hesitate. Never have I entered the cabin without permission. Jabbart prods me in the back. "Find it," he whispers, glancing over his shoulders to see if any of the crew has awakened.

I light the wall sconce and a pale yellow light fills the room. I move quickly to the Captain's desk, remembering how he had rolled up the Letter and placed it inside the middle drawer. I reach far inside and my hand curls around a roll of parchment. When I pull it out, the gold ribbon wrapped around it glitters in the dim light.

"Here is the proof we need," I say, sliding off the ribbon and spreading the Letter of Marque open on the desk.

Jabbart looks over my shoulder as I begin to read the document aloud. I am halfway down the page when Jabbart snatches the document from the desk for a closer look.

"What?" I ask, alarmed.

"Read the dates, Jameson," he says slowly, handing the letter back to me.

I run my eyes quickly down the page until they find the date the document was drawn up —almost three years ago. Near the bottom of the page, beneath Queen Anne's signature, is another date—the day the Letter of Marque expires. I murmur the words aloud. *This agreement holds true until January 1st...the Year of our Lord 1713."*

"Lord help him," Jabbart whispers. "On the day of the battle, the Captain had no authority to act. He fired on the merchant under an expired order."

I grab the Letter of Marque and roll it up. "We will take it to Constable Smythe and explain that the Captain had no knowledge of the treaty. Surely he will understand that the Captain has been a long while at sea and could not have known."

Jabbart laughs, but there is no humor in his voice. "Did he understand that you picked up the bread in the bakery because you were starving?"

"The Captain has served our Queen well; the constable will consider that and set him free." I reply.

"His loyalty to Queen Anne matters not," Jabbart says. "If the constable determines that the Captain committed piracy, he will make him pay the price."

A chill runs up my back. "How so?" I ask.

"Hanging," Jabbart says. "Come market day next, a noose will be slipped around the Captain's neck, and he will swing."

CHAPTER TWENTY

Jabbart and I leave *Destiny* before dawn the next day. Cook is on deck preparing breakfast when we leave; he watches us ready the longboat, but he doesn't ask questions. We say nothing. It is better no one knows of our plan.

Jabbart guides the longboat across the harbor through the stinging rain. I stay at the other end of the boat, one hand on the pocket in which I placed the Letter of Marque. All night, it lay open beside me. More than once, my finger traced the signature sweeping across the parchment, as grand as a peacock's tail. My heart pounds as I think of what will happen if the plan I have conceived goes awry. I pray God it works. If not, the Captain will hang, and it is likely that Jabbart and I will swing beside him.

As we approach the center wharf, I pull my hat down low on my brow. The wool shirt I wear feels itchy against my skin. Jabbart and I found it yesterday while rummaging through the crates in storage for new garments that would not bring as much notice as royal uniforms. Sweat trickles down my back— an odd feeling on a chilly, wet morning.

"Keep your head down and let me talk," Jabbart says. He grabs a post at the end of the pier and pulls the boat to the dock. I note the empty wharf with satisfaction. We are early enough that Charles Towne still sleeps. By midmorning the harbor will be crammed with vessels and the piers crowded with people. Had we come later, slipping unseen into the town would have been impossible.

After we have tied up the boat, we head down the beach toward a secluded part of the harbor lined with fishing shanties. I peer from beneath the brim of my hat, wondering that Charles Towne looks so different to me after my months at sea. My mind turns back to auction day, when I was led through these streets with my hands tied before me. I bowed my head then, too, ashamed to be recognized as the printer's son turned bread thief. If I were able, I would walk through Charles Towne wearing the Queen's colors and holding my head high.

Near Fishers' Alley, the overwhelming stench causes bile to rise in my throat. Grimacing, I hold my breath as I quickly sidestep a pile of rotting fish heads that are covered with flies.

Seeing my discomfort, Jabbart chuckles as if he smells nothing out of the ordinary. "You get used to such smells after a while," he says. "The taverns are not far now."

"Good," I say. "My stomach pleads for food."

"Mine as well." He jingles the coins in his pocket. "We shall dally beside a fire this day and fill our bellies. Then we'll slip back to town."

I'm surprised I can talk of eating when I am so nervous When I think of what we must do, I feel ill. The plan came to me as I stood at the Captain's desk, staring at the worthless Letter of Marque. I pray we can pull off the dangerous deed.

We stop at a tavern that is close to the water. The hinges have rusted on the door frame and a split in the middle of the oak door allows the candles burning inside to show through.

"Are you sure this is it, lad?" Jabbart asks, his hand upon the door.

"Aye," I say, glancing up at the sign. "This is Mr. Carver's place, for sure."

"The old lady might be dead by now," Jabbart says. "Then what?"

I don't answer because I don't know what will happen if old Netty Nottingham is no longer indentured to Wilton Carver. I last saw her when Carver led her away from the auction block. The old woman's back was bent and her steps wobbly. Had she survived the past year working in a place where wet sea winds swept over her daily? Moreover, if she did remember me, would she think of me kindly and help me with the plan?

A crackling fire burns in a corner hearth, filling the small tavern with dense gray smoke. My eyes burn as I count the empty tables. We have come at the right time; the fishermen are still out on the water.

A door near the back swings open suddenly. Wilton Carver stops, surprised to see that he has guests so early in the morning. I turn away quickly and make a show of warming my hands before the fire.

"Is it breakfast you'll be wanting?" Carver asks. "My cook has just risen, but she can bring bread and such in short order."

"Aye," Jabbart responds cheerily. 'Tis bread we want, and goose eggs, too. The sea winds have chilled us to the bones."

The tavernkeeper grabs the iron poker beside the hearth and gives it a hearty thrust. "Surely a pint or two of ale will warm your blood."

"Surely," Jabbart said. "Perhaps three or four pints; we have nowhere else to be this day."

Biting back a smile, I move closer to the fire. When we dressed that morning, Jabbart insisted we wear the fanciest clothes we had found. The ruse has worked. Carver noticed the expensive clothes and thinks we have pocketfuls of coins.

"Sit close to the hearth whilst I fetch your ale," Carver says, brushing away crumbs from the night before. He gives me a fleeting glance before he leaves. When the door stops swinging, Jabbart whispers, "You can't keep your head bowed all day like you've done something wrong. It will surely raise an eyebrow if you act like a criminal."

"I fear he will recognize me," I say. "He used to come to my father's shop."

"You've grown two inches since I first laid eyes on you, and the sun has roasted your skin the color of weak tea. Your sleeves pull tight against your muscles now. You look nothing like the pale, sniveling boy Ferdie dragged onto the deck that first day."

"We'll know soon enough," I whisper as the door swings open again and the old woman I met in jail comes through carrying two tankards of ale. She slams the platter onto the table, causing the ale to slosh over the sides of the cups. Our early arrival does not sit well with her.

"'Tis a wait you'll have for the eggs," she announces. "One person I am and an old one at that. You've come at an ungodly hour; the eggs are still beneath the hen!"

I raise my head and stare into her face. She hasn't changed much since I last saw her, except that she has lost more teeth. Taking a deep breath, I reach out and touch her arm. "Lord keep you, ma'am," I say softly, repeating the words she whispered to me on auction day.

She tries to snatch her arm away, but I hold it. I lean toward her, so that her eyes can search my face. She bends closer, straining to see through the smoky haze around the table.

"Lord keep you, ma'am," I repeat slowly.

Suddenly, a gap-tooth grin spreads across the old woman's face. She clasps her hand down over mine. "That He has! As He has surely kept you!"

CHAPTER TWENTY-ONE

Y ou shouldn't have come back," the old woman says. "You're a posted runaway."

"I know, but something has happened that forces me here."

"Are you in trouble again?"

"It is a story that cannot be told quickly."

Netty glances over her shoulder. "Carver left for the pier to wait for the fishers to return. Tell me why you've come." She looks at Jabbart as if she is just noticing him. "And who is this man you've trusted with your life?"

I quickly explain about being taken aboard *Destiny*. The old woman's eyes narrow when I tell her about Ferdie clouting me on the head.

"When I heard you'd run, I prayed for your safety. I never thought you'd been taken by Attack Jack."

"It was by accident that Ferdie grabbed me, but the Captain would not let me leave the ship. I have served as a sea artist for Queen Anne."

Netty takes a gulp of the ale she brought for me and urges me to continue. I tell her about the attack by the Spanish merchant and the damage to *Destiny*. I explain about tossing the food overboard and sailing to Crossed Island for repairs. When

I tell her about the cave flooding and Solitaire Peep drowning, her eyes light up. "'Twas a viper, that one," she says.

"No," I say. "He did not deserve to drown. I would not have left the cave had I thought I could save him."

The old woman hobbles to the back door and looks out at the alley. "Get what you need and be on your way, boy," she says. "'Tis not safe here. You look full-grown now. They will not treat you kindly if you're caught."

"They did not treat me kindly before," I reply. "What difference will it make that I am a few inches taller?"

"Your neck is still short. If they catch you, 'twill be stretched long—like a Christmas goose."

I sigh. "As the Captain's neck will be soon, unless we can help him." I explain about the arrest and the expired Letter of Marque.

At the end of my story, the old woman draws back with a skeptical look on her face. "'Tis an act of piracy to be sure," she says. "The Governor has issued a declaration that all pirates are to be hung and their heads stuck on a pike near the harbor."

The very thought of this sends a chill up my spine. "No," I say. "We fought the Spanish merchant in defense of Queen Anne. Besides, we were fired upon first. If a pirate is amongst us, it is the captain of the Spanish merchant."

"You must save yourself, lad. You cannot help Attack Jack. Only a letter from Queen Anne could set him free."

"And I shall present such a letter," I say. "That is why I came here to see you."

A clanking in the kitchen causes the old woman to leap to her feet. "My master's back. At midday, he goes into the cellar to check his ale. We can talk then."

A short while later, Netty comes out carrying a tray of steaming eggs that have been fried in fat, half a loaf of bread that has been toasted and smeared with stewed plums, and two thick slices of salted ham. I start to speak to her, but she gives a quick shake of her head. "'Twill be two shillings, six pence," she demands, looking over her shoulder.

Jabbart counts out the coins and drops them into her outstretched hand. "A pot of tea to wash it down would be welcomed," he says loudly. "Tell your master we are grateful for his good service."

After she serves our tea, we do not see her again for the rest of the morning. At noon, she comes back out. "He has gone into the cellar," she says. I invite her to sit while I continue with my story, but she refuses. "If he catches me at your table, we're all done for," she whispers. "He'll see that we're not strangers to one another." She touches my hand and leans forward. "Be quick and tell me what you need."

"First, we need answers," I say, asking the question most on my mind. "Does Carver still visit my father's shop?"

"The new printer and Carver are like this." The old woman crosses her fingers one over the other.

"Can you tell me the printer's habits?" I ask. "Does he leave the shop often?"

"Most nights he comes here to drink the ale Carver serves him in exchange for free printing. He's as cheap as—"

I break in. "Will he come here tonight?"

Netty shrugs. "'Tis likely, but I cain't say for sure. Perhaps near suppertime."

"Then we'll wait and see," Jabbart says. "If God wills it, the printer will come this night."

The old woman frowns, confused. "What does it matter if he comes here?"

I bite my lip. I trust her not to betray me, but having one more person know the plan makes it more dangerous. I wait until Jabbart gives a nod of approval.

"If he comes," I tell her, "Jabbart and I will leave here and return to town. At midnight, when the town crier snuffs the street torches, I will enter my father's shop and print a new Letter of Marque."

"The printer may not tarry that long," Netty says. "Some nights he stays for hours, others he's gone after one tankard."

I glance at Jabbart. "I cannot do this quickly. I will need most of the night."

Netty thinks for a moment, then grabs my arm. "Never you mind, lad. If the printer comes, you'll have the time you need. I shall pour him double ales and seat him close to the fire. His head will droop soon enough. When he wakes, a new day will be upon him."

The door swings open suddenly and Wilton Carver beckons to his servant. "Why is it that you tarry out here so long?" he asks. "The dishes from this morning are not yet scrubbed."

"'Tis our fault," Jabbart says quickly. "We asked her if it might be possible to have roasted hen for dinner with new potatoes and onions. Our sea journey has been long and our bellies beg for something more than dried fish and hard biscuits."

"Then you will be staying until late?" Carver asks, a smile forming on his face.

"Perhaps," Jabbart says, "if there is reason to do so."

Turning to the old woman, Carver says, "Go wring a chicken's neck and pluck the bird clean."

Complaining loudly, Netty stomps off to the kitchen. Jabbart smiles broadly. "My son and I thank you for your good hospitality. We'll be pleased to rest our weary bones a while longer beside your fire."

Carver nods. "A storm is blowing in. I can think of no better place for you to be this day."

"Aye," I say loudly. "We shall spend the day and perhaps

the night, too." With these words, I lift the tankard of ale. "When I return to ship, I will share the story of this fine day in Charles Towne." Setting it down without taking a sip, I offer a silent prayer that I might live long enough to do just that.

CHAPTER TWENTY-TWO

With the wind blowing hard and the waves swelling, the fishermen leave the water early. Some stop by the tavern on their way home. Each time the door swings open, I bow my head and watch through the lock of hair that falls over my eyes. From time to time Jabbart's chin falls to his chest, but the fear of being recognized keeps me awake and alert.

When the moon appears, Netty comes from the back room to fetch our dishes and the roasted chicken carcass that Jabbart and I have picked clean to the bones. She stacks the dishes and slowly wipes our table with a damp cloth.

"I don't think he's coming," I whisper. The supper hour has passed. Most of the customers have wiped the ale from their chins and gone home.

"'Tis growing late, for sure," she says, glancing toward the door. "Might be the rain's keeping him home tonight."

"Isn't there another way, lad?" Jabbart asks. "Can't you use the pens and inks the Captain gave you?"

I shake my head. "We'd fool no one that way. To try would be begging the hangman to knot the rope around our necks."

Tossing payment for our dinner onto the table, Jabbart stands. "We should head back to the ship," he says. "'Tis no use waiting anymore."

I try to swallow my disappointment. I had been foolish to think we could pull off such a deed. Still, I couldn't help but wonder what might have happened had I been given the chance.

"What will become of you, boy?" The old woman whispers. "When Attack Jack swings, where will you go?"

Jabbart places his hand on my shoulder and squeezes hard. "The constable will likely seize *Destiny* as a pirating vessel, but I will see the boy to safety. If luck is with us, we'll secure a place on another ship sailing far from here."

I stare at him in disbelief. "Surely you do not want to give up on the Captain now? We will find another way."

"We have no choice," Jabbart insists. "The constable will pronounce sentence as soon as the trial is over; there is no time to do else."

"If the Captain hangs, you must flee without me," I tell him. "Gunther is right; I've brought the devil's luck to *Destiny*."

The old woman makes a sour face. "You spew superstitions, boy," she says. "Do not waste your breath speaking such nonsense. If the devil's luck is on that ship, you can—" She stops midsentence as the tavern door swings open. A great gust of wind blows across the room, extinguishing several candles.

"'Tis him," Netty whispers. "He has come!"

Standing in the doorway is the printer, his hair wild from the wind and glistening with rain.

I draw a deep breath. "Aye, the silver-bearded man," I whisper, my voice taut, "who has stolen what is rightfully mine."

"Careful, lad," Jabbart cautions. He touches my arm lightly. "Do not let your anger spoil what we've planned."

Snorting, the old woman whispers, "'Twould take a hurricane to keep that vulture from drinking the free ale."

The printer steps inside, standing in the doorway while he scans the room. Hurrying over, the old woman shuts the door behind him. "I've the perfect table by the fire," she says, her voice loud and cheery. "Warm your bones a bit whilst I fetch the ale."

The printer looks at her with a raised eyebrow. "Would the table be about to collapse?" he asks. "Surely that is the only reason for your kind offer."

She laughs merrily at his joke and taps his arm. "Come and sit whilst I fetch your tankard."

Still looking suspicious, the printer makes his way to the table. Taking off his overcoat, he tosses it onto a chair. He sits down and looks around the room, rubbing his hands together to warm them. When he sees me staring, he nods slightly before looking away.

"'Tis clear he doesn't recognize you, lad," Jabbart whispers. "He didn't give you a second glance."

"Only because he is not expecting to see me this night," I say. "Surely he has not forgotten so easily the one he robbed."

"Pray God he has," Jabbart says. "'Twill make our task easier." He nudges me as the old woman comes through the door and heads straight to the printer's table.

"My master is serving a strong brew this day to ward off the chill," she says, placing a dripping tankard before the printer. "Taste and see for yourself."

Wiping the brim of the mug with his sleeve, the printer takes a long drink. He smacks his lips to show his pleasure. "'Tis fine, to be sure, but my stomach growls. What's left in your pot tonight?"

"A treat," the old woman says. "Roasted chicken and potatoes. Let me fetch you a trencher."

Before leaving the room, she stops by our table. Bending low as if wiping it clean, she says, "I'll see that he has a long wait before tasting a morsel. All the while, I'll pour him double ales."

"Keep him here as long as you can," I urge. "I must work until dawn."

"Begone, lad," the old woman says, glancing around to see if we are watched. "I shall pray that your plan works, for I would hate to watch the hangman's hood cover your flaxen hair."

My eyes meet hers. "I shall not forget the kindness you have shown me this night and before."

With the slightest smile that only I can see, the old woman turns away.

Jabbart and I step out into the night, letting the door bang shut behind us.

Outside the tavern we button our collars high onto our necks against a pounding wind.

"There's no one about on the wharf," Jabbart says. "'Tis the best luck we've had yet."

"Aye," I reply, tucking my chin to my chest. "Who else would be out walking on such a night?"

We don't speak again as we make our way back toward the harbor. I think about what lies ahead. In my mind, I see myself enter the print shop with its small front door and four windows that look out onto the street. I imagine myself standing before the type board, my hands brushing against the cold, metal letters as I pick the ones I need. Then my mind goes blank, for I have not thought beyond that moment, have not imagined what might happen if someone discovers me there.

The town crier announces the ninth hour as we reach the print shop. Candles still burn low in the windows of nearby homes. I stand silently before the door. The sign my father painted has been removed and an engraved one hangs in its place.

"Pinkerton," I say in a voice that can barely be heard. My voice shakes, but I read the sign aloud: "Samuel Pinkerton, Printer and Recorder."

Jabbart places his hand upon my shoulder. "Do not forget why we are here, lad," he cautions. "One cannot change what has already happened. Save your anger for another day."

For a moment, I want to rip the sign from its chain and fling it to the street. But I know Jabbart speaks the truth. The print shop has already been stolen from me, and there is nothing I can do about it.

"Another day, then," I murmur, my hand upon the door. "I shall stand on these steps another day."

Looking up and down the empty street, Jabbart turns the knob slowly, pushing against the door. "'Tis locked tight," he says, frowning. Up until that moment, I had not considered what we would do if the thieving printer had locked the door behind him. I hold my breath as Jabbart pulls a dagger from his pocket and inserts the tip into the lock, twisting it from side to side. The lock clicks loudly as the knife finds its mark. Jabbart pushes on the door and it swings open.

Stepping across the threshold, I whisper to Jabbart, "I will open the shutters on the bottom window. If you see someone approach, tap against the pane to warn me and then move into the alley."

Jabbart sticks his hand into his coat pockets. "Work as fast as you can, lad, for surely I will freeze if you don't."

"Surely you will hang if I don't," I say. With those words, I enter my father's shop and pull the door shut behind me.

CHAPTER TWENTY-THREE

I allow my eyes to adjust to the darkness before moving into the type room. I don't need a candle to lead me to the sectioned type board where the metal letters lie, each in its own space.

Standing before it, I breathe deeply, savoring the smell of the metal type, the taste filling my throat. I brush my fingers against the top row, knowing instinctively which letter follows which, feeling my way along until I near the end. My hands stops at *Q*, and I pick up the top letter and place it aside. Then my fingers move down the board to *U*. I remove a lowercase letter and place it alongside the *Q*. My fingers flying, I go back down the board to the *E*s and then to the *N*s. Picking the type comes naturally, and I work quickly, pausing only to light a small lantern near the board. I pull from my pocket the expired Letter of Marque. My eyes move continually between it and the type board as I choose the letters needed to create a new copy.

Selecting the type doesn't take long; I once spent hours doing the same for my father. The harder task comes when it is time to place the letters between the wooden railings that will hold them straight so they can be inked. My fingers feel clumsy as I work in the narrow space, and more than once I drop a letter onto the floor. Rather than take the time to look for it, I leave it and pull another.

Finally, I stand up straight and stretch. My back aches from bending over the board. The pain vanishes as I survey what I have done. A new Letter of Marque, dated one year hence, lies before me. Pride washes over me as I hurry to the cabinet where my father kept the inks.

When I reach the ink cabinet, I tug on the silver handle, but the door is locked. My stomach sinks as I move about the room, pulling open drawers and running my hand along the shelves. Not one bottle is to be found. I feel myself beginning to panic. I glance nervously at the window. Is it my imagination, or is the sky lighter than it was a few moments earlier?

"What would my father do?" I say aloud, though I cannot recall a time when my father ever faced such a moment. Then an idea comes to me, and I look around the room for the small pots of ink that my father used for signing documents. I discover a small crate of them beneath a table near the window, along with a small box of silver-nibbed quills.

As I ink the type, I think fleetingly of the printer. Does he still sit at the table before the fire, or has he started the walk home? Had the old woman been generous enough with the ale?

After applying ink to the last row of letters, I blow gently on them to dry them quickly so they do not stick to the parchment. Then, placing the paper over the type, I lower the board and press down with all my might.

Praying silently that nothing has smudged, I wait a few minutes and then lift the board. My breath catches as I look down on the new Letter of Marque. "Identical," I whisper. Not even my father would have been able to tell the difference between the two.

My heart pounding with excitement, I open a fresh bottle of ink and dip the silver-nibbed quill into the pot. Staring hard at the Queen's signature, I steady my hand above the parchment. Then, with a sweeping motion, I sign Her Majesty's name to the new Letter of Marque. Stepping back, my eyes fill as I look at what I have done. I wish my father were beside me and that we were gazing upon the Letter together.

As I begin to clean up, it occurs to me that my father would not have approved of the forgery. I had no choice, I reason. Without this document, the Captain will die. And if the plan fails, he still may. I quickly pour ink from bottle to bottle, balancing each so that it won't be easily noticed that they were opened. By the time the printer discovers the empty bottles, *Destiny* will be far from Charles Towne. "It was the right thing to do," I murmur. Then I repeat the words aloud, as if someone else is there to hear them.

I am wiping the ink from the last letter when I hear a hard tap against the window. I thrust the dirty rag beneath the table and slam the cover board down. After returning the roll of parchment to its place in the corner, I run to the window and pull the shutters closed. I quickly survey the room, looking for any sign that I had been there half the night. Everything appears as it should. With the new Letter of Marque tucked inside my jacket for safekeeping, I make my way to the back of the shop.

Jabbart appears as soon as I open the door that leads to the alley. "Be quick. The merchants are emptying their slops. They will soon open for business."

"What of it?" I say, my voice smug with satisfaction. "In our fine clothes we look like two of Charles Towne's finest citizens."

Jabbart snorts. "Fine citizens, indeed! I am sopping wet, and your hands are splattered with black ink."

I hold my hands out in front of me. Even my fingernails are tipped black. "I had to work quickly," I explain with a sigh.

"No matter," Jabbart says, beckoning for me to follow. "Stuff your hands in your pocket and let's hurry, lad. We must be across the harbor before it fills up."

We see no one until we start to untie the boat from the wharf. A man appears, but he continues on down the pier, his mind elsewhere. As we row toward *Destiny*, I replay the day's events in my mind. Surely Gunther is wrong; no one with the devil's luck could have accomplished what I had that day.

It is only when I step onto the deck of the ship and see spots of silvery gull droppings upon the polished wood that I remember the metal letters I dropped onto the print shop floor. In my haste to clean up, I forgot to retrieve them and place them back on the type board. My face must have shown my dismay.

"What is it?" Jabbart asks quietly.

"The letters," I say. "I dropped some and forgot to pick them up. They lie beneath the board where they fell."

Jabbart smiles with relief. "Is that all? Surely a printer drops a letter now and then."

"Perhaps," I say doubtfully. "But a real printer, a good printer, picks them up and returns them to their place. A printer's letters are like gold to him."

"You did a fine job this day," Jabbart says. "Now stop worrying about such a small thing and go below and sleep. Tomorrow is the day before court. We still have much to discuss when you wake."

In the storage room, I remove my ink-stained clothes. Wrapping my blanket around me, I sink down on the pallet. My mind drifts from the tavern to the print shop with its new sign upon the door. "Another day," I murmur as sleep quickly overcomes me.

CHAPTER TWENTY-FOUR

The next morning, I rise early and wash from head to toe, scrubbing my ink-stained hands with salt until they are red and stinging. I dress carefully, buttoning the collar of my shirt up to the neck, and polishing the brass buttons on my coat. I replace the rigging I used for a belt with a leather strap I found in one of the crates. I pull back my hair with a ribbon borrowed from the Captain's cabin and tuck it beneath my hat so that only a few strands are visible.

Jabbart smiles when he sees me and says I am every bit a royal sailor. After we eat a hurried breakfast, he rows us across in the longboat. Before he finishes tying the boat to the wharf, all eyes are upon us. He has warned me to be prepared, confident that the news of Attack Jack's arrest will cause much excitement amongst the townspeople. As I climb from the boat, I force myself to return their stares with a disdainful glance of my own, hoping that the royal uniform I wear will keep even the boldest from approaching.

With the hour of trials almost at hand, the harbor and streets are jammed, and merchants have set up tables near the courthouse.

"'Tis like a fair day," Jabbart says, amazed at the excitement. "Surely they must know that this day brings death for some of the accused."

"Their memories are short," I reply, remembering how my father's friends had turned their eyes from mine on auction day.

The sun casts a glare against the cobblestones, and I place my hands above my eyes to shield them as we walk toward the courthouse on Main Street. I have been inside the one-story building only once with my father, when he made a delivery. It contains a room for holding trials and a smaller room with barred windows where the accused are kept until it is time to approach the magistrate's bench.

A crowd has formed out front. A low murmuring begins as we shove our way into the building, but no one challenges our right to enter. I hear a few men mutter the Captain's name. Jabbart has guessed right; the charge of piracy against a royal officer has caused a stir. No doubt half of those present have come hoping to see Attack Jack get his comeuppance.

A fire in the hearth warms the main hall. We rub the chill from our hands in silence and wait for the trial to begin. From time to time, I pat my coat pocket to reassure myself that the new Letter of Marque is still there.

At exactly noon, the courthouse bell rings, signaling the jailer to march the prisoners to the courthouse. I draw a deep breath and think about what lies ahead. Will the magistrate believe the Letter has just been found? Will anyone recognize me as the indentured servant who disappeared a year ago? I wipe my clammy hands against my breeches.

When the crowd's excitement reaches a pitch, Jabbart and I turn toward the door. The crowd parts to allow the prisoners through. Many of the townspeople hold scented cloths to their noses to ward off the smell of the filthy prisoners. Some of the men shove them as they pass.

I clinch my teeth when I see the line of prisoners. Most have their heads down, defeated and weary from their stay in the jail. There is one woman, the rest are men.

"Where is he?" I whisper. The procession of prisoners has ended and the Captain is nowhere to be seen. Alarmed, Jabbart looks about. Then, the sound of clanking irons fills the hall and the Captain, separated from the rest of the prisoners, is led to the front of the line.

"They've shackled him like a mad dog," I say angrily.

"Aye," Jabbart replies. "'Tis normal for a prisoner as famous as he. Still, they have not broken him." Unlike the other prisoners, the Captain holds his head high, a bored look upon his face.

"'Twill soon be over, lad," Jabbart says, pointing to the magistrate, who has taken his position behind his bench. "It appears that they want to hang him this day."

I cover my mouth to whisper. "I shall not step forth until they ask for evidence of innocence. We do not want to give them time to think about why we have come."

Jabbart nudges me toward the front of the room. "Go in closer, but don't show yourself until the last moment."

I swallow hard and take a deep breath. My stomach and legs feel weak. When the magistrate bangs his gravel calling for order, I move quietly to a position near the bench.

"Bring forth the infamous Attack Jack," he says eagerly, as if he has long waited for such a moment.

His shackles clanking loudly with each step, the Captain moves to stand before the bench. In a defiant tone, he speaks first. "You have wrongfully accused a loyal officer of the Queen. I demand you release me this moment."

The magistrate bangs his gravel. "You will speak only when addressed. You have no authority in this court."

"When Queen Anne hears of what you've done," the Captain says, "you will rue the day you called for my arrest."

Laughing, the magistrate shuffles his papers. "'Tis Her Majesty's wish that we hang all pirates. From the documents you've produced, or should I say, have *not* produced, you fit that description."

"The document you seek is on my ship. Were I able to get it, I would prove I am not a pirate."

"There is no need," the constable says. "Your commission to act on the Queen's behalf is on record. 'Tis clear it was expired when you boldly attacked the Spanish ship."

"The Spanish captain fired first; I did not seek a fight."

"Then you admit you fired upon the Spanish ship?"

"I fired to protect the property of Queen Anne and for no other reason."

Looking around the room with a wry smile, the magistrate replies, "With an expired Letter of Marque, you no longer had authority to act in her name. As an experienced captain, surely you know that!"

Some of the onlookers applaud the magistrate's challenge. Jabbart, who has slipped through the crowd to my side, nudges me. "He has fallen into a trap by admitting he fired upon the enemy ship. It matters not who fired first."

The magistrate bangs his gavel again. "You cannot refute the charge of which you are accused. Acting under an expired Letter of Marque, you fired on a Spanish merchant. By doing so, you have broken the Treaty of Utrecht and shamed our Queen. And for that you will hang." He looks around, smirking. "Unless, of course, there is someone present who can prove your innocence."

"Now!" hisses Jabbart, urging me forward.

As I make my way to the bench, an excited murmur fills the room. I glance at the Captain only long enough to see a look of astonishment on his face.

"I have the proof you seek," I say, pulling out the Letter of Marque.

"What is this?" the magistrate says, his voice tight. "What tricks do you seek to play on this court?"

I hand over the document. "I have brought the Letter of Marque. Proof of the Captain's commission is before you."

"And who might you be?" the magistrate asks haughtily.

"A royal sailor, sir, in service to Queen Anne aboard her ship, *Destiny*."

"You lie to save your captain," the magistrate says. "And for that you will hang beside him." He unrolls the document and holds it close before him. When his eyes fall on the dates at the bottom, his face darkens.

"This cannot be," he says. "The records we have do not match what you have produced."

"Records are slips of papers and nothing more, sir. Surely our Queen's signature overrules all else."

The magistrate scans the letter again. Clearly confused, he bangs his gavel down hard. "Send the constable to bring the printer," he says. "He must vouch for the document's truth."

Though my legs go weak, I smile as if this suggestion is ridiculous. "Our Queen's signature sweeps across the page. Is that not proof enough?"

"Perhaps," the magistrate says. "If the printer vouches for Queen Anne's signature, your Captain will indeed go free. But God pity you both if the printer finds it false. Your arms and legs will be pulled from your bodies and displayed with your lying heads for all to see." Waving me away, he calls for the next prisoner to be brought forward.

"We are done for," I whisper to Jabbart. "The printer will surely remember that he did not set such a document."

"Pray hard, lad. The guards have locked the doors. No one is permitted to leave until the printer speaks."

By the time the printer is found and brought to the courthouse, four of the accused have learned their fates—one to go free and the other three to serve terms in prison. When the printer steps into the room, all conversation stops. He makes his way to the bench.

The magistrate hands over the Letter of Marque. "You have been called to verify the signature across the bottom as that of Her Majesty, Queen Anne."

Taking the letter, the printer rubs his chin, clearly enjoying the importance placed upon him. He reads the letter carefully, his eyes scanning the page and then going back to the top. As he reads, a bewildered look appears on his face.

"He cannot figure it out," I whisper to Jabbart. "It looks valid, but he does not know how it came to be."

"He must say it's the Queen's signature," he says. "Anything else and the Captain will swing."

The printer clears his throat. "I cannot say if this is an official royal document."

I rush forward and snatch the Letter of Marque from the printer's hand. "Surely you need spectacles," I say, waving the paper before his face. "The Queen's signature is spread across the page."

Startled, the printer opens his mouth to speak, and then quickly closes it. His eyes meet mine, and I see a flicker of confusion within them. Frowning, he stares at the letter and then at me, as if he is trying to sort it all out.

I speak quickly. "As Charles Towne's printer, you must be able to recognize the Queen's signature."

"Aye," the printer says slowly. "As a printer, I have seen it many times."

I press on. "For if you could not recognize it, then your worth as a printer could come into question. You might even be called a fake."

The man draws back. "No one would dare call me a fake." His eyes meet mine and hold them. "Only one willing to die would do so."

I let the silence grow between us. When I finally speak, my words hold a challenge. "You must tell the magistrate if this document bears our Queen's signature. If you cannot say yes or no with certainty, then we must ask how such an unskilled man has joined so noble a trade."

Reaching for the Letter of Marque, the printer makes a show of looking closely at the document. He grimaces in concentration and holds the document up as if he is trying to see through the parchment. Finally he says, "Aye, 'tis the Queen's signature for sure. Only she writes in such a fashion."

The magistrate leaps up. "Only a minute ago, you could not say. Now you speak as if there is no doubt!"

"With a closer look, I can say for certain that Queen Anne, and only Queen Anne, penned this document." Turning to face the onlookers, the printer says, "Such is valid proof of the accused's innocence."

Without waiting for the magistrate to speak, the Captain steps forward and addresses him. "The Queen's work has been delayed long enough. Perhaps, sir, if you are quick to undo the wrongs here, I shall speak more favorably of you when I visit her court."

The magistrate forces a smile. "My apologies for the troubles placed upon you my good sir. I will secure the proper papers and see that you are released upon the morrow."

"My duties to our Queen have been delayed long enough by this court's error," the Captain says. "I think it would be wise to expedite this matter."

There is a long silence while the magistrate considers what action to take. I find it hard to hold my tongue, but I wait.

Finally, the magistrate sinks back into his chair and places his gavel on the table. "Very well," he says. "I will ask my guard to unfasten your irons and escort you to the wharves immediately."

I hold my breath until the shackles fall from the Captain's wrists. Then, with my eyes straight ahead, I fall into step behind Jabbart and follow the two of them toward the door.

After the guard who has seen us onto the ship turns away,

the Captain claps me on the back. "You are to be congratulated on carrying out the finest of all ruses," he says. "After we pull anchor, you must tell me all."

I smile. "There's not that much to tell, sir."

Jabbart laughs. "At sea and on land the lad has proved himself worthy to be called a royal sailor. Were it not for his printing skills, we would not wake to see the morning's sun."

I hear him, but I don't answer, for I am looking back toward Charles Towne, watching until those on the wharves become invisible. A gull flies overhead, swoops low, and then heads off across the sea.

Aye, I think. *A royal sailor perhaps, but for sure a printer's son.*

CHAPTER TWENTY-FIVE

The moon has already appeared when I drag the net back over the railing. The lightness of it tells me that once again the sea has refused to share with us. Sighing with disappointment, I kick it open to see if there is anything to fill Cook's pot. Three fish, two that are as still as night, lie before me. Cook, who is waiting impatiently at my side, grabs the fish that is flopping around and tosses it into the bucket. Frowning, he stares at the other two that still have not moved. I pick both of them up by their tails and am about to fling them into the sea when Cook grabs my arm. "Keep them, lad," he says. "My pot is almost empty."

I stare at him incredulously. "Surely you cannot think we will eat dead fish?" I say. "We will all be bent over the railing before nightfall, spilling our guts into the sea."

"'Tis only stunned they are," Cook says, pulling the fish from my hand. "You dropped them too hard onto the deck."

"No," I reply. "They are as dead as those that rot on Charles Towne's shores after a summer storm. It would be foul to eat them."

Frowning, Cook pushes his thumb into the belly of one of the fish, drawing back quickly as it bursts open and shoots forth a thin green liquid with a smell so rank that I clamp my hand over my nose and mouth. Hesitating only a second,

Cook tosses both fish over the railing. "Throw out the nets again, lad," he growls as he hobbles toward the hatch.

Obeying him, I hurl out the nets and watch as they float beneath the water. Then I grab the swabbing stick to clean the mess from the deck. As I work, I try hard not to think of my empty stomach, for I have not had a full meal since the evening at Carver's Tavern. When I think of the food that once filled our storage room, it is hard to believe we have come so low. Though we had not yet filled our hold with food, we pulled anchor on the night of the trial and sailed quickly away beneath a crescent moon. The Captain did not push for a Letter of Credit from Queen Anne, for he said it was best not to linger and flaunt our victory over the magistrate and provoke him to make inquiries.

After we were safely at sea, Cook brought ale to the Captain's cabin, and Jabbart and I spent most of the night there, telling the Captain how we came to save his life. He gazed upon the new Letter of Marque with amazement, unable to distinguish between the old and the new, except for the dates. Cook said 'twas good luck the old woman fed us chicken on a night of rain, for had she served us pig or cow, the Captain's neck would now be stretched long and thin.

The Captain has set us on a course back to Crossed Island, a safe place, he says, to make plans for the future. With Queen Anne's War ended and Peep dead, I sense he feels a loss that cannot be put into words. When we beach, Cook says we must go deep into the woods to hunt more wild pigs and to search for wild onions and fungus stalks to flavor the food. For now, we are on quarter rations, which is barely enough to keep the hunger pangs at bay. This morning, breakfast was two biscuits and a small piece of cheese per man. The flour is alive with weevils, but Cook does a good job at picking out most of them, and only twice at breakfast did I feel their crunch beneath my teeth.

My second net yields one large fish with a wide gray body that resembles a horseshoe. Its tail is long and pointed, with a tip as sharp as a needle. The fish flops around on deck, swishing its tail back and forth until Cook spears it with his dagger and it lies still. Cook lifts the fish up by its tail and holds it up for all on deck to see, grinning as if the sea has yielded a piece of gold.

There are a few grumbles at supper, but not many, for the Captain commands Cook to bring forth a small barrel of rum. Cups are passed all around as the fish is ladled into our trenchers. By the time the moon appears, most of the crew is snoring upon the deck, their cups still in their hands. My stomach rejects the sour taste of the brew. A fire spreads between my ribs after I swallow, so I drink only a few sips. Not ready to go below, I stay up on deck to watch the moon rise. Cook says that sometimes the man who lives within will appear, and the one who is first to see him is granted one wish.

It is peaceful now that Gunther is gone. The Captain says it is likely that he learned of the piracy charge, and fearing that he too would be accused, ran off to seek another port where he might find work. His gunnery skills are known far and wide, so he will not be without a ship for long. From time to time, I catch Ferdie throwing looks my way, but without his friend to back him, he leaves me alone.

Tonight, my mind drifts back to the cave on Crossed Island, and the moment when Peep was swept away. A wet breeze blows off the water, and I shiver hard, for it reminds me of the sea spilling over me inside the cave and the look on Peep's face when the water pulled him away. I cannot help but think that had I gripped his hand harder, Peep would be with us today. The Captain says I must not dwell on the past, but instead, look to the future. I hear his words, but as one who was trained to record my memories, I cannot always abide by his advice.

Before I head below to sleep, I steal one more glance at the moon. I am startled to see a dark form in the middle. Leaning over the railing, I lift my face to the sky and whisper only two words into the wind to be carried upward to the man who watches me.

"Solitaire Peep."

CHAPTER TWENTY-SIX

It is not quite noon the next day when I see a large shadow looming ahead. I lean far over the railing with the eyeglass tight against my face. A thick fog rises off the water, blurring the lens. Rubbing the glass against my shirt, I lift it for another look. When the cliff that conceals the cave appears, I lower the glass quickly and turn away. I have no desire to look upon the place that took Peep's life.

Ratty Tom calls out land, and Jabbart clangs the bell to signal all men to come on deck. Soon the deck is swarming with crew. Two men drag forth the anchor, while others climb the rigging to adjust the sails so that the ship does not go into shore too fast. Jabbart is at the tiller, yelling at Ferdie that it is too soon to bring out the longboats. A few minutes later, the Captain comes through the hatch. Seeing the cave in the distance, he smiles. "It is always a good sight to see when we first approach Crossed Island."

"Still?" I ask. "Even since the storm?"

The Captain nods. "You do not know this, lad, but it was Peep who first discovered the cave. Only once have I been inside."

I can't hide my surprise. "And yet you let him take the maps there?"

"Aye, there was no safer place."

I don't answer. How could the Captain think the cave was safe? Had it been truly safe, Peep would not have died.

The Captain moves closer and leans low so that no one else can hear. "When we beach, Jameson, you must lead me to the maps."

I shake my head quickly. "I cannot remember the way, sir. All that day has become a blur in my mind."

"Then you must clear your head and think hard. We cannot tarry long on Crossed Island. The winter winds push hard at our backs, and we must set sail for England before ice forms in the water. It is a long journey."

"England!" I exclaim, shocked that the Captain would even consider such a voyage after what just happened in Charles Towne.

"Aye," he says. "I will seek an audience with Queen Anne and learn what my future holds."

"Begging your pardon, sir, but surely you cannot be thinking clearly," I say. "By then, she will have learned that you fired on the Spanish merchant without permission, and she will call for your head on a pike."

"Then you think me a pirate, too?" the Captain asks, raising a brow.

"No, but you have broken the Treaty of Utrecht, and I have forged the Queen's name to lie for you. When word reaches our Queen, I fear for your life...and mine."

"That is why we must take her the maps," the Captain says. "Queen Anne has penned her name to the treaty, but her thirst for new shores will not die. When she sees all that the New World offers, she will quickly forgive us."

"England," I repeat. I had never imagined making such a journey. For the rest of the morning, until the order comes to drop anchor, I go about my work repeating the word in my head. *England!*

By nightfall we have cast anchor close to shore and set up camp on Crossed Island. When dusk falls, I gather dried willows for Cook's fire. I stroll along the beach thinking about all that has occurred since my parents' deaths and the day I walked onto the auction block. It is hard to believe that so much has happened to me in so little time.

Cook feeds us a meager meal. The Captain makes light of it, saying that come morning he and I will go deep into the woods to hunt more wild pig, while the rest of the crew cast nets from the shore and scrape the rocky shoals along the beach for shelled fish.

As the night deepens, I pull my pallet close to the fire, remembering the mosquitoes that plagued me before. I take out my artist's kit and begin to draw a picture of us, a ragged and hungry crew sitting around a roaring fire with our cups filled with ale. I sketch our humpbacked Cook poking at the fire to bring it to life. I gently splatter ink upon the page to resemble the embers that float upon the air. I dip my quill deep into the black ink and let the pen flow lightly across the paper, sketching the Captain's hair in long wisps so that anyone who gazes upon my drawing will know that a strong wind blew off the sea this night. I dip again for Ratty Tom and Ferdie, who huddle shoulder to shoulder, each clasping his cup with two hands, silently staring into the fire. I do not show it to anyone when the ink is dry; instead, I carefully roll up the parchment and place it with my things that I brought from the ship. While no words fill my page, I am content that I have captured one moment that I can look upon someday. In my mind, I will be able to travel back to this place where the stars glitter against a black sky and willows sway in the wind.

As the fire dies and the crew drifts away, I unroll my mat. The cool breeze and the crackling fire make it easy to fall asleep. But soon I am dreaming of Charles Towne. I am tied to the end of Strabo's line, heading to auction. Then suddenly, I am clinging to the ratlines while sharks circle beneath me. The wind blows so hard, my fingers won't hold the lines. I clutch tighter, but I begin to slip, and there is nothing I can do. As I fall into the ocean, I bolt upward. Gasping for breath, I look about. The crew sleeps soundly beside Cook's fire.

"Only a dream," I whisper, running my fingers through my hair. A strong wind blows off the water, and I shiver and wrap my arms around my knees. The visions had seemed so real.

I sleep again, this time deeply. Before I know it, I hear a commotion around me. Morning has dawned and I am surprised to see that I am the last to rise.

"Good that you slept late," Cook says, prying open one of the oysters from a bucket that someone has already brought to him. "I watched you toss and turn half the night."

I nod, but say nothing.

He pokes me gently with his stick. "Look alive, boy, for today we will hunt the wild pig."

"We?" I ask, surprised to learn that Cook would accompany us.

"Aye," Cook replies nonchalantly. "The Captain says everyone is needed to fish and trap food. The others are already out with the nets. Using the tip of his knife, he scoops three oysters from their shells into a trencher and hands it to me. "Eat them raw, lad, for you'll need the strength they'll bring."

Remembering the taste of the wild boar on my tongue, I tilt my trencher and quickly slurp up the oysters, not minding their fishy flavor. I am wiping my mouth on my sleeve when the Captain comes up behind me. "Are you both ready?" he says. He pulls out two muskets he has tucked into his belt and hands them to Cook and me. I take mine gladly, for I have no desire to fight another wild boar by hand. When Cook turns away to toss sand on the fire, I whisper to the Captain, "Will Cook come with us to the cave?"

He nods. "With Peep gone, I will need someone to help you get the maps to Queen Anne if something happens to me. Cook has promised me to do that."

"What might happen to you?" I ask, my voice rising in alarm.

He lifts his hand to calm me. "I only mean that it is good to prepare."

I am surprised when the Captain says we will take one of the longboats to the other side of the island and get the maps before we begin hunting. I want to ask why we wouldn't first hunt for food, but the Captain seems lost in his thoughts this morning. I imagine that his mind will not rest until he knows that the maps survived the storm and that he will be able to prove his worth to Queen Anne.

The Captain steers the boat, and Cook and I row out to just above where the waves break so that we are not tossed back to shore. Every now and then, Cook stops rowing and bends low over the side, whispering to the fish to come to the surface. The Captain says nothing about the delay he causes, and I am beginning to think that he believes there is some truth in Cook's superstitions.

Before midmorning, we are within sight of the cliff. When I see it ahead, I take a deep breath. The Captain turns to me and, seeing my face, places his hand on my shoulder and squeezes lightly. "Look not to the past, for you can change nothing there; it is only the future you can mold." Nodding, I push the oar harder into the water and direct the bow of the boat toward the massive gray rock.

We tie the boat loosely in a thicket of reeds on the shore. I wade out as I remember Peep doing, grabbing a handful of the vines that dangle over the opening of the cave. The Captain follows behind me, turning every now and then to check on Cook. The water is up to Cook's neck, and for once he is silent as he struggles to keep his mouth above the waves. I wonder if he thinks that perhaps there is something inside the cave that could fill his pot, for surely not even duty to the Queen would make him risk drowning himself.

The inside of the cave is dark, but there are no shadows dancing upon the walls as there were the night of the storm nor is there the sound of the rushing sea that filled my head to near bursting. Instead, I hear only the faint drip of water from places beyond where I can see. The smell of slime fills my nostrils. Cook complains that he cannot take time to scrape some from the walls to take with him. The slime found in caves, he says, is good to rub upon aching gums.

We have not walked far when the cave splits into two paths. The Captain stops and turns to me. "Which way to the maps, Jameson?"

Uncertain, I look around, struggling to remember which way Peep and I went on the night of the storm. Had he gone straight, or had he veered off to one side? When we walked out, had we turned left before the water rushed through, or had we turned right?

"I can't be sure of the way," I whisper, embarrassed. "The walls all look the same to me. Peep led the way in; I just followed." It had not occurred to me to pay attention to where I was going. Peep had been the one in charge, the one who knew the way. I had simply followed along like a child on a walk, not bothering to take note of our path.

"You must try to recognize something," the Captain says. "This cave stretches for a great distance. If you can't remember the way, the maps will be lost forever."

I don't want to tell him that I think the maps are lost, that the sea had already claimed them.

Cook sits down to rest while the Captain and I walk ahead and try to decide which way to go.

I run my hands along the wall, straining to recall something that will lead me to the hiding place. I close my eyes and force myself to remember the night of the storm. I see myself kneeling at the base of the wall, struggling to dig deep enough so that the maps will be safe. Peep is standing above me ranting, and I hear him yelling my name, shouting loudly above the wind. So strong is the memory that I jump when the Captain squeezes my shoulder. "Did you hear that?" he asks, looking around.

"What? I whisper. "We are the only ones here. Who else would know of this place?"

"I heard it meself," Cook says, rising from the floor and hobbling toward us. "'Twas the bleat of a goat, for sure. And she called the boy's name!"

"Could it be our lost goat?" I ask, listening carefully. "Perhaps she wandered in and became lost."

"It could only be our goat," Cook replies, his eyes wide. "'Twas a full moon last night and lost goats are summoned by full moons. 'Tis likely she called your name, too, for a full moon brings out strange powers in four-legged animals."

I snort. "Goats cannot talk, full moon or not! I think you make up most of what you say."

Cook lets out a great roar, and for a moment, I fear I have offended him. I open my mouth to offer an apology, but Cook is hobbling away from me faster than I would have thought possible. I yell for him to come back, that he'll get lost if he goes deeper into the cave, but he ignores me. His arms are stretched out before him as if someone is commanding him to come forward. The Captain starts after him, and I follow.

Then suddenly my feet refuse to take another step. I open my mouth, but the name I want to shout lodges in my throat. I am frozen, unable to do anything except watch and pray that I am not imagining things. When the light from the lantern hits his face and I see the gleam of his jeweled eyepatch, I know for sure that the man walking toward us with the goat at his side is Solitaire Peep.

When Peep reaches the Captain, he drops the leather satchel at his feet with a grin. I watch, stunned, as the Captain grabs him in a tight hug, and then holds him at arm's length and stares at his face as if he cannot believe his one-eyed mate stands before him. Cook hobbles and leaps around in circles. Turning to me, Peep says, "James-me-son, surely you didn't think I would have left the maps after the sea swept through, did you?"

I sink down onto the floor and run my hand across the leather satchel. A long moment passes until I find my voice. Looking up, I say, "When you were swept away, I tried to go after you, but the water was rising too fast. I would not have left the cave had I known you were trapped.

Solitaire Peep scowls. "Trapped? Use your noggin, boy. There are more openings than the one we climbed through. I stayed in the cave until I was sure the maps were safe."

I look over at the Captain. "Did you know he had escaped?"

"Not until we approached the island yesterday and I saw smoke coming from the cliff. It occurred to me then that Peep might have survived. I didn't want say anything in case I was wrong."

"But I saw land first," I protest. "I looked through the glass and saw only fog."

"You must think like a sailor, boy," Peep says. "You saw not fog, but the fire I lit. Best learn the difference between fog and smoke, or you may find yourself trapped forever on an island someday."

I sigh. I want to tell Peep that sailing is not natural to my blood like it is to his, and that perhaps I will never learn all the tricks that come through living a sailor's life. Instead, I smile and pat the goat on its head. "You were right, Cook," I say. "Lost friends are surely summoned by a full moon!"

Leaving Crossed Island
The Year of Our Lord 1713

We are two days sail from Crossed Island, with a strong wind beneath full sails. The crew is strong and our hold full of smoked fish, turtles, and wild pigs. The Captain says we will sail first to Port Royal to sell some of the clothes in the crates below deck and purchase the rest of the supplies we will need for our voyage to England.

From hereon, I intend to sketch daily what lies before me so that when we reach England, the Captain can show our Queen all that awaits her to command in the New World. I pray she will be pleased with my work and reward the Captain with a new commission to sail in her name. It is a mighty world that lies beyond Crossed Island and Charles Towne, and the Captain says I must seek it with him and Peep.

One day, I will return to Crossed Island. Already, I long to feel its fine-grained sand beneath my feet and hear the rustling of willows on the dunes. There is still much to learn about the island. Peep will not say exactly how he escaped from the cave. I ask from time to time, but his only reply is that my nose is too long.

Last night, while the others slept, I pulled out the parchment on which I had written of my days in Charles Towne's jail. I am grateful when I read the lettering on the pages and feel the raised marks from the ink. Though I may never follow in my father's trade, his gift of lettering is one I shall have always; it is a powerful feeling to know my memories will never be cast into the wind.

—JMC

ACKNOWLEDGMENTS

A huge thank you to my family, particularly my husband Jerry, who believed in me and this story, and my sons, Gerard and Keith, who had to share me with Jameson for a good long while. Thank you to my mother, Jean Connors, who read a very rough manuscript and offered positive feedback, and my sister Jeannie, who never once rushed me off of the phone when I wanted to read "just one paragraph" to her. I'd also like to acknowledge my brothers, Jimmy and Tommy, native Floridians who answered numerous vague questions about beaches and wildlife without realizing they were helping me out.

A heartfelt thanks to all of my friends who patiently listened to me go on and on about pirates and privateers; I hesitate to try to list names in fear that I might leave someone out, but you will recognize who you are when I say these conversation filled our nightly walks around the block, our daily phone conversations after the kids left for school, our beach days, and our weekly drives to the mall.

To my agent, Caryn Wiseman of Andrea Brown Literary Agency: thank you so much for having faith in this story and for your advice and relentless efforts on its behalf. The journey was long, but you never gave up.

To the editorial staff of Peachtree Publishers, and particularly Kathy Landwehr, thank you for selecting my book and for your efforts in bringing it to fruition. Kathy, your gentle approach in asking questions or making comments made the editorial process a breeze for me. I am still in awe of your keen eye for consistency with details.

And finally a special acknowledgement to my fifth grade teacher whose assignment to compose a story using the weekly vocabulary words ignited my passion and love for writing. That I can still recall writing the story and reading it to the class speaks of what it meant to me.

—Susan Verrico